RUNNING STEER RANCH

JAMES BOXSTAL

CONTENTS

CHAPTER 1

John Daniels looked out the window of his cabin on the Running Steer Ranch. *Looks like rain. Let's hope our guests don't mind getting wet* . He chuckled to himself. He remembered how one of the guests screamed when she saw a rattlesnake.

He told the woman that it wouldn't hurt her unless she bothered it. The woman's husband looked like he was going to faint when it raised its tail and rattled louder. John just shook his head and told them that the snake was just warning them that they were too close. He led the guests away from the snake.

Of course, then Max heard about it, and I got told to look out for the guests' happiness and safety. Like I don't do that all the time anyway. John's smile faded becoming a scowl at the fact he was working on a Dude Ranch.

John moved away from the window and left his cabin. Walking across the sandy Nevada land combined with the

wide open spaces took the tension from his shoulders. *Better to spend my days wiping city folks' noses than being stuck in some damn factory.*

Halfway to the oversized mess hall, the tension returned to his shoulders. The manager of the Dude Ranch, Max Coleson was hurrying to cut him off. *Great, what did I do now?* Gritting his teeth, he took a deep breath forcing his face to relax by the force of his will. *I need this job.*

"What's up Max?" John's voice managed to be civil if not friendly.

Max stopped a couple of feet in front of John, his face flushed and breathed heavy. "Never seems to get cooler, does it?" He took off his Stetson to wipe his forehead.

If you weren't carrying around that extra forty pounds of gut, you wouldn't be bothered by the heat so much. John stood waiting for Max to catch his breath and get to the point. While they were never friends, they both knew that the manager job should have gone to John.

"Corporate is having a woman from one of Chicago's largest radio stations come out here. They are spending a

couple million on the new advertising campaign." Max sounded excited and smiled like the news was a gift for John.

John grunted. "Don't you mean they are buying advertising for their fifteen new Dude Ranches across the

Midwest and East Coast?" John raised an eyebrow waiting for Max to admit the obvious facts. The Running Steer Ranch was barely breaking even during tourist season. Other times well they lost less money than they had before Max took over and cut the budget to the bone.

Max's face lost the smile. "She is going to help us get more guests out here. Corporate insists that she get the full experience." The edge in Max's voice was a warning.

I know where this is going. A woman in her forties alone. John knew he was still decent looking. He didn't know that the women, which came out to watch him put on the bronco riding and horseman show at the end of every two weeks stay at the ranch, they were interested in watching his lean five-foot eleven-inch frame get sweaty more than anything else.

Max put his Stetson cowboy hat back on. "I need you to show her around and help her learn what sort of guests we

cater to. If she doesn't have a good time, then we very well might all be out of jobs."

John nodded. "Sure. I can make sure she is included with the current group of tourists. They have already been here a week, but she should catch on. After all, she is from Chicago."

Max was already nodding, all smiles once more. "Good. Good. I am sure with your help; she will understand why being here is the best vacation for people." Max turned on his heel and walked in the direction of the office.

John watched him get halfway there before he continued on his way to the dining area. Walking around to the side, he looked in. Since Max took over as manager six months before, the ranch hands had to eat and drink all their meals with the guests.

Good all clear. I timed this just right. All the guests are out with Roger riding around the south pasture. He went inside and grabbed himself a cup of coffee, looking around at the large room filled with plush chairs and tables polished to a high sheen.

Max should have listened to me. People come here to be in the old west. The cappuccino machine and omelet bar just ruin the atmosphere. He walked over to his usual table where a few of the other ranch hands were sitting.

"Morning John. Did Max tell you the news?" John nodded at the stable hand, Dalton Martinez. Dalton thought of himself as a ladies' man. In his early forties, balding and with a beer belly, his ladies were only in his head.

"Yep." *Shit, I should have just taken my coffee to go.*

"What do you think she looks like? We have a bet going on that she is blond, tan and with her nose so high in the air, clouds move in and out of her nostrils." Dalton paused, chuckling at his own joke. When no one else joined in, he asked, "What is your wager?"

John rolled his eyes. "I am not getting suckered into one of your ridiculous bets. I have already been told off by Max. So I do not care what she looks like."

"Damn, I was just asking. No need to bite my head off." Dalton turned back to his breakfast. John sat down beside him and sipped his coffee.

"I see that all of the guests aren't here for breakfast. Did they all go with Roger for the ride in the south pasture?" John asked.

"They went on one of the trails with Casey. He pestered Max until he agreed to let him show the wild horses to the guests." John turned to see one of the trail guides, Gary Tanner standing behind him.

"Why would Casey do that? He knows that the trail to the wild mustangs is treacherous. That idiot!" John slammed his cup on the table just as Casey Maxwell walked in the door. Still covered with trail dust, he led the guests he had taken to see the horses into the dining hall. John stomped over to Casey.

"Hey, John. What's up?" Casey wearing his Wrangler shirt and jeans, complete with a huge gaudy belt buckle. Casey was everything John despised about dude ranches. Blond hair, green eyes and unlike Dalton, he had a string of ladies.

Somehow, Casey always pushed John into the angry rages he thought had been left behind when he stopped drinking years ago. This time, John didn't care who saw his anger. It wasn't even a month ago that Casey had taken a single mother riding. While he 'entertained' the young mother, her seven-year-old son fell down an embankment and broke his leg.

"What in the hell did you think you were doing!? That trail is for experienced riders only. You were damn lucky with the last stunt you pulled only ended up with a child having a broken leg!" John was a foot away, breathing hard trying not to lose his temper completely. His sleeveless t-shirt was clean and showed his well-defined biceps as he clenched his fists.

Casey slouched and smirked at John. "If you want help with ladies John all you have to do is ask."

Seeing red, John grabbed Casey by the front of his shirt and shook him. Casey's mouth fell open in shock, and he turned pale at the animal rage in John's eyes. The door opened again as soon as the guests had moved away from the fight unfolding before them. A flash of a camera and the sound of a shutter were the only sounds in the dining hall.

Mackenzie Tucker walked into the dining hall. The male guests and all the ranch hands, except Casey and John, turned to stare at her. The Armani Collezioni pantsuit was pressed to perfection. The stiletto heels added three inches to her height. Sighs filled the room as she removed her Gucci sunglasses.

If she was upset to see one man shaking another and a fight about to erupt before her, it did not show. *Well, so this is west. No different than the honky tonk Susannah had dragged us to for her bachelorette party.*

With a sigh, she used her weight to slam the heavy door as hard as she could. The resulting boom echoed through the room. As the few eyes that had not been staring at her turned toward her, she placed her hand on her hip. As she did so, the mid length skirt rose. The exposed calf was toned, tan and smooth under her pantyhose.

The slim almost petite Gary moved into the silence, tugging on John's arm. "John, let go of him." A second tug and Casey slipped back onto the bottoms of his feet. "The guests are fine."

John grunted but stepped back from Casey. He ran a callused hand through his thick dark hair. Turning away, he moved over to pick up his worn cowboy hat from the peg by the door. *Never should have left it here last night. Just got tired of answering the guests' questions.*

Gary followed him, keeping an eye on Casey to make sure he wouldn't take a swing with a new woman in the room. "The kids are frightened." Gary nodded drawing John's attention.

The only answer John got from Gary was a half grunt half snort of derision as John glanced at the kids. *They don't look scared.*

Seeing Casey smoothing his wrinkled clothes and already smiling at the new woman in the room, Gary hurried towards her. "Hello, Miss. Sorry, you saw that. I'm Gary, one of the trail guides."

"Mackenzie Tucker," Mackenzie smiled thinly at Gary before looking around the room. Turning, she half opened the door to leave.

"You wouldn't happen to be the woman from the radio station, would you?" Gary asked, stepping smoothly in front of the door. When Mackenzie stepped back with a nod allowing the door to close, Gary called, "Hey John, come over here a minute."

Well if you had a shower and I had a bottle of wine you sure could make the evening interesting. She shook her head dismissing her brief fantasy before it could even get started. *Never going to happen. I should already be on my way to the Royal Palm Casino to get them signed before Shiyoto Media beats me to it.* They had already stolen one multi-million-dollar account from her that year.

Taking her eyes from his wide shoulders and thick tanned arms, she looked him in the face as he drew closer. "Are you John Daniels?" When he nodded once, she continued. "You're supposed to escort me around today."

John nodded his head again. He remained silent and waited. A frown started on her face as she tried again. "I need a tour so I can get this contract wrapped up. I have an appointment and should already be on the road."

He opened the door and held it open for her. With a sigh, she went back into the desert heat, and he followed her. As she stood squinting in the bright sunlight, she then put her sunglasses back on while John walked in the direction of the stables.

She followed at his heels. *Maybe he is mute. Damn cowboys, always trying to act tough. I need to get this over with.*

John glanced at Mackenzie from the corner of his eye. *Damn, she is really in shape. You do not get in that shape just sitting behind a desk.* She looked to be about his age with startling emerald eyes. Her dark brunette hair was pulled back in a bun, but a few wisps escaped from it.

As a light sheen of sweat spread on her forehead from the heat, she did what she was good at; she went on the offensive. "So do you always pick up your employees and shake them or was this a special occasion?" John stopped, and Mackenzie stepped past him before coming to a stop.

"He put people's lives in danger. Children's lives." He looked her in the eye challenging her to find fault with his actions. *Go ahead keep pushing me this morning. I can find another job.* He ignored the fact that the taxes on his Grandpa's ranch were due again in a few short weeks and that jobs anywhere were hard to come by. Especially when all you had for a resume was cowboy as your job description.

"So you're not mute." Mackenzie watched as John took a deep breath and walked past her toward the stables. She turned to follow him but had a hard time as she tried to keep up with him. *Why did I have to wear heels today? I knew I was going to be on a ranch.* She stopped just in time to avoid running into John again.

"These are the stables," John announced standing in the door blocking most of her view. "Do you know how to ride a horse?" His voice was half challenge half sneer.

"I went to a summer camp when I was younger where they had horses and they taught us how to ride them."

John's shoulders relaxed at her words. "At least you know how to ride. That will make the next few days easier." The slight mellowing of his posture and eyes changed him back into the alluring man she had half-fantasized.

"Wait." She protested as he started taking a saddle from where it hung over the first stall door.

"Don't worry. I see Chestnut is still in her stall for some reason. She is a good horse for an experienced beginner rider." John did not turn to look back at Mackenzie as he placed the saddle over the door of Chestnut's stall and went to get a bridle.

How do I get myself into these messes? Mackenzie stepped a couple of feet into the barn relaxing despite herself. The smell of horses, clean straw, and a faint lavender scent filled her with a strange longing. Shaking herself, she focused on John's back.

"Actually, I think I have about seen enough. Thank you anyway, I will just head back to Max's office and wrap things up." Mackenzie said, stepping forward instead of back.

John looked back at her with a raised eyebrow. "Max said you were to be part of the current group of guests. He wanted me to get you ready to spend the next two days with them."

A mare with big inquisitive brown eyes stuck her head over the stall and nickered in John's face. He ignored her, pushing her head back idly while he continued to watch Mackenzie, who as if sleepwalking took another step. She was now only a couple of feet from the stall and John.

"I really do have to go. I have lost a large account to one of our competitors already this year and can't afford to lose another one." She stood leaning forward as she finished speaking. *Why did I tell him all that?*

John opened his mouth and at that moment Chestnut used her nose to dump the heavy saddle off her stall door and onto John's foot. John's mouth opened wider, "Shit that hurts!"

"John! We do not use that kind of vulgar language in front of guests." Max stood sweaty faced in the barn doorway.

John was standing holding his foot. Mackenzie hid her smile by stepping forward and patting Chestnut on the nose.

Chestnut nickered, pushing her nose farther out so Mackenzie could reach the right spot.

John straightened wincing as he stood on his booted foot again. "The saddle landed on my foot." While there was no apology in his voice, it was civil if a bit on the gruff side.

"She is a guest and shall be treated as one. Corporate just confirmed she will be staying. You have today and tomorrow to get her ready to finish with the current group's stay." Max stepped forward, handing papers to a frowning Mackenzie.

"I was supposed to take Blaze and work with him." John's protests cut off Mackenzie's own.

Max shook his head. "I have already given that task to someone else. This is more important than the horse." Max lowered his voice, stepping closer to John while Mackenzie was busy reading the papers he had given her. "If anything goes wrong, they will be replacing both of us."

John nodded, not trusting himself to keep a civil tone now. Damn, I have been working with that stallion for months. He was my chance to get back in the rodeo.

Mackenzie folded the papers up, and Max handed her a key. "Here is a key to one of the guest cabins. Let me show you where it is right quick while John gets Chestnut ready. Follow me." They left the stables, leaving John with Chestnut.

Chestnut stuck her face in John's and snorted. John frowned and wiped his face. He then smiled and patted her nose.

"You knocked that saddle on my foot on purpose, didn't you?" Chestnut just looked at him and shook her head. John bent down and picked up the saddle. He placed it back on her stall and grabbed her bridle. He placed that on her head and led Chestnut out. He placed the saddle blanket and then the saddle on her back and cinched it on. Then he led her outside, tied her to a pole and tightened the cinch after Chestnut let out the breath she was holding. He then went back inside the stables to get his horse, Blackjack ready.

Mackenzie looked in the one small suitcase she had brought with her. *Why did Jacob tell them that I was staying longer than what we had agreed upon? I am so unprepared for this, and I hate being unprepared.* She took another look in the suitcase and closed it. *The only thing I packed was two business suits, my workout outfit, and a dress along with my makeup and hairbrush.* She sighed and sat down on the bed beside her suitcase. She looked over at the oak nightstand and noticed a little brochure. She picked it up and read through it. *Good, they have a gift shop. Maybe they have some clothes I can wear while I'm here. I'll find it tonight. Right now, I need to get changed and go for the tour around this huge place.*

John leaned against the rail of the corral with his hat

pulled over his eyes, waiting for Mackenzie to show back up. He heard someone approach but did not look up. The person stopped in front of him, and all he could see was a pair of dark red shoes and two sweatpant legs. He looked up slowly until he found himself staring at an emerald-eyed woman with her dark hair in a ponytail.

"Well, I am ready to go on that tour now, Mr. Daniels," Mackenzie smiled as it dawned on John who she was.

She watched John to see what he would do next. When he just stood there, she smiled and held out her hand. "I forgot to introduce myself to you earlier. My name is Mackenzie Tucker." John reached out and shook her hand. Something akin to a little shock ran through their hands as they touched.

"Pleased to meet you, Miss Tucker. As you already know my name, there is no point introducing myself. I work here as a cowboy guide which means I make the guests feel as if they are cowboys. At the end of their stay, I do a little bronco riding as well as a barrel race. Me and a few of the other ranch hands all have a barrel racing contest for the guests to watch."

"So how long have you been working here?" John kept silent. *If this woman knew the real reason I am not in the rodeo anymore, she would refuse to help us get the advertising Corporate wants.*

Mackenzie frowned when he remained silent. *Fine then.*

Don't tell me. Mackenzie walked over to the horses. John moved to help her get on Chestnut, but Mackenzie was already on her. He stared at her in surprise.

"I told you that I went to a summer camp where they had horses."

"Do your stirrups need adjusting or are they just right?" asks John.

"They seem to be the right length for me." states Mackenzie.

John shook his head and climbed onto Blackjack.

John led Mackenzie to the cattle corral. He pointed out theLonghorns and other cattle that were in the pen. "We have Longhorn cattle, Angus and Belted Galloway."

"So what do the guests do with the cattle?"

"We take the guests on a cattle drive to the border of Oklahoma and back here. They have a lot of fun. It lets them feel like they are real cowboys. The kids especially like it." Mackenzie liked the way John's eyes lit up when he was talking about the cattle drive.

"So did you do any of this stuff when you were growing up?"

John smiled sadly. "My grandfather took me once. We had fun. I liked sleeping under the stars. That was the summer before I started high school." His voice trailed off at the end.

Mackenzie wondered why talking about his grandfather

taking him on a cattle drive made him sad. She decided not to push him to tell her. John led her away from the cattle and showed her the chicken coop. He explained that the kids loved feeding the chickens. Next, he showed her the field where they let the cattle and horses out to graze.

After a few minutes, John turned Blackjack around. "I have to teach the kids a lasso lesson which starts in two minutes. Let's head back." John flicked the reins of the bridle and took off with Blackjack. Mackenzie turned Chestnut around and followed.

She caught up with John. "I am having trouble getting Chestnut to go where I want her to go. Hopefully, it will come back to me." John shrugged and took the reins from Mackenzie. He led them back to the stables.

They both dismounted and led the horses into the stable. John led Mackenzie back to Chestnut's stall and showed her how to undo the saddle and where to put it, the saddle blanket and the bridle. He then put Blackjack in his stall and unsaddled him. He brushed Blackjack down and filled his water bucket. He left the stall and couldn't find Mackenzie. Then he heard her laughing outside.

He found Mackenzie talking to Gary. John clenched his fists and then realized what he was doing. *Why do I feel like punching Gary? I have no problem with him ever. I mean Gary likes men.* It dawned on him a few seconds later. *Oh my God! How can I be jealous of Gary? I just met this woman, and now I have feelings for her.* John shook his head to clear it and then walked over to them. He noticed that the horse corral was already set up for the lasso lesson.

"Hey, Gary. Did you set the corral up?"

"Oh hey, John. Sure did. Figured you could use the help."

"Thanks, Gary."

"No problem. See you later." Gary left and went to the dining hall. John turned to Mackenzie.

"That was nice of Gary to set everything up for you." Mackenzie looked at the little bales of hay with the fake horns attached to them.

"It is. Usually, if I am busy with something else, Gary always would set up the hay bales for the kids to practice on. Sometimes he will start the lesson if I couldn't get away from what I need to get finished." John noticed some of the parents coming over with the kids. "I need to get started. Why don't you watch what the kids have learned so far? Maybe you might learn something while you watch the kids learn."

He turned to face the kids who had come to learn to use a lasso. He smiled and started the lesson. Mackenzie watched as the kids stood in the corral, holding their lassos while John demonstrated a new technique with his. The kids watched in awe as he threw the rope at one of the hay bales. The rope slipped over one of the fake horns and the kids as well as Mackenzie clapped. Mackenzie left the horse corral and walked to the office.

Mackenzie looked back as she was halfway to the office. She watched as John smiled and made the kids laugh at something he said. *He seems to be good with kids.* She sighed and continued walking to the office.

CHAPTER 2

"That is the plan for getting you your advertising on the radio. Now that I have seen the ranch and know who the potential clientele is, perhaps you could tell my corporate office that it is all set up for the advertising." Mackenzie leaned back in her seat and waited for Max to comment. Max frowned and got up from behind the desk.

"I'm sorry Miss Tucker, but corporate wants you to have the full experience. To get the perfect feel for this place. You must see the day to day activities and all that we have to offer."

Mackenzie frowned. *It was worth a try. Why did they have to do this to me? I really need to beat Shiyoto Media to the casino deal.*

Max offered Mackenzie his arm. "Well, it is dinner time.

You don't mind walking to the dining hall with me, would you?"

"Not at all, Mr. Coleson." Mackenzie got up from her chair and followed Max to the eating area.

They entered, and Max led her to the table where some of the other guests were sitting and pulled her chair out for her. Mackenzie saw John sitting with some of the kids and making them laugh. John glanced over and smiled at Mackenzie. She smiled back, and he walked over to her and Max.

"Where did you go? One minute you were watching the kids learn to lasso and the next you were gone."

Max frowned. "She was with me going over a few things." John nodded and walked to his usual table. He ate and watched as Max left and the guests Mackenzie was sitting with introduced themselves. She smiled and answered their questions but seemed a little out of it. She took one look at the food and frowned.

John chuckled to himself. *Probably not used to eating this kind of food. Probably eats out every night.* John shook his head and continued to eat his food.

After dinner, Max had all the men get a fire started in the big fire pit in the front of the main office. Mackenzie watched as John picked up a few logs to put on the fire once it got going. She saw that all the kids were excited. She smiled and went to search for the gift shop.

John watched as Mackenzie walked away from the campfire. He caught up to her.

"Need any help?"

"Actually, yes. I need to find the gift shop."

John held his arm out to her. "Here, let me escort you. Don't want you falling in the dark." Mackenzie could barely see the grin on his face in the dark. They walked in silence to the gift shop.

Once they got to the gift shop, John held the door open for her. Mackenzie waved at Gary, who was behind the counter.

"Good evening, Miss Tucker. What can I help you with?"

"I need a few outfits for my visit. All I packed was mostly business suits. Now I need clothes that will make me feel like a real cowgirl."

Gary smiled. "We have just the right clothes." He led her and John to the woman's clothes. "Here we are. Take your time, Miss Tucker."

"Please call me Mackenzie. It will be much easier than calling me Miss Tucker while I'm here."

"Alright," Gary smiled and left them to man the counter again. Mackenzie went through the racks looking for clothes in her size. John reached into the rack and pulled a shirt and pair of jeans.

"Here, try these." Mackenzie looked at the clothes John had picked out and moved to another rack.

It is hard finding clothes for myself. Usually, I have Janine buy my clothes for me. Mackenzie perused the rack and found a pair of slim-legged pants. *Nice, I finally found something to wear, and they are in my size.* She continued looking through the racks and found some decent looking shirts in her size. *They're not the best, but they will have to do.*

Mackenzie turned to John. "I think I found plenty of clothes to last me for the rest of my stay. Thank you for all your help, Mr. Daniels."

"You can call me John if you want. Most of the guests do." John smiled, and she smiled back.

He's got a nice smile. He should smile more often. She shook her head at herself. *Why did I think that? I need to make it through the next few days so that I can get to the Royal Palm Casino and close that deal.* She sighed and went to the counter to have Gary ring her purchases up. John held the door for Mackenzie and walked her to her cabin.

"Why don't you join us at the campfire, Miss Tucker? It is considered to be the best part of being here according to previous guests."

"I would like that. Thank you. You can call me

Mackenzie too if you want." John nodded as Mackenzie unlocked the cabin and placed her bag of clothes inside. She locked it back up, looped her arm through his, and they walked to join the others at the campfire.

CHAPTER 3

The next two days passed by quicker than Mackenzie had expected it.She couldn't believe that tomorrow she would make it to Royal Palm Casino in time to close the deal. The other guests talked nonstop about the bronco riding and barrel racing contest that were scheduled to happen that evening. Mackenzie was unsure about it, however.She did discover that she enjoyed learning to be a real cowgirl. She still had trouble using a lasso, though. John was very patient with her and the other guests who also had trouble with the lasso.

She didn't like the fact that the trail guide, Casey was constantly trying to get her alone. That seemed to be the only low point of being there. However, it always seemed that Gary was there to save her from Casey. Mackenzie was grateful that Gary was so helpful despite the fact that she could tell that Gary liked other men.

Around lunch time, Mackenzie walked to the dining hall along with a few of the other guests. She had made friends with some of them, and the kids seemed to enjoy her company.

They arrived at the dining hall and found a note on the door.

Today we are having lunch where the campfire pit is.

Mackenzie could smell what could only be hamburgers and hot dogs. She smiled. *That smells delicious. I'm used to smelling hot dogs cooking in Chicago, but these smell much better than the hot dog vendors' hot dogs back home.* She followed the guests to the campfire pit and saw John manning the fire and cooking the hamburgers and hot dogs. He saw Mackenzie and waved to her. She waved back.

"Good afternoon, Miss Tucker. How are you doing today?" Mackenzie turned to the voice and found herself face to face with Casey.

"Afternoon, Mr. Maxwell. I am doing fine. I'm looking forward to going on the trail after lunch."

Casey smiled. "Please call me Casey. Anyway, they have

the other trail guide Kevin work that trail but he wasn't feeling very well this afternoon, so I'm taking over."

Mackenzie nodded and moved closer to the campfire. She didn't like the way Casey looked at her. It still creeped her out.

John watched as Mackenzie moved away from Casey. He shook his head. *It was always the same. Anytime a beautiful woman would arrive at the ranch by herself; Casey would befriend them and try to get them to sleep with him.* John went back to flipping the hamburgers.

"How's it going over here?" John turned and saw Mackenzie standing beside him.

"The hamburgers are almost done. The hotdogs are on that table there if you want some. We also have some chips over there too."

"What about drinks?"

"Usually, we don't serve soft drinks, but Max thought the kids and adults might like a treat to go with the burgers and hot dogs. We have bottles of water as well." Mackenzie walked over to the table, grabbed a plate, a hamburger bun and a bottle of water. She walked back over to John.

"I think I will wait for the burgers to get done. I've never had a grilled hamburger before."

She watched as John flipped the burgers one more time before he yelled, "If anyone wants a hamburger, line up behind Miss Mackenzie!" The kids all rushed over and stood behind her.

One of the kids tugged on Mackenzie's jeans. "Miss Mackenzie, do you like hamburgers too?"

Mackenzie laughed and leaned down. "I never had one before, but I'm willing to try it." The little girl laughed and Mackenzie hugged her. She straightened and found John staring at her. She blushed as he grinned and placed a burger on her bun. She walked back to the table and put pickles, onion and ketchup on it. She found a bag of kettle chips and walked over to one of the blankets that were set up for the guests to sit on.

After John was done serving the people who wanted hamburgers, he fixed his plate and walked over to Mackenzie. He noticed that Gary had joined her at her blanket. Gary was sitting beside Mackenzie, who was laughing at what he had said.

"What's so funny?"

"Gary was just telling me about the time one of the kids from before I got here had tripped while playing tag with the other kids and landed right into Gary's lap," John remembered that day. The kids were running around, acting like little monsters. The kid in question had tripped on his shoelace and fell straight into Gary's lap. Gary had been sitting down on the ground eating and the kid face planted into Gary's mashed potatoes.

Gary and John shared a grin as they remembered how the kid cried because he had mashed potatoes on his face. The kid's parents tried hard not to laugh but to no avail.

John sat down on the opposite side of Mackenzie. He noticed that she still had her hamburger on her plate. He took a bite of his own and saw Mackenzie take a bite of hers as well.

"So how is it?"

Mackenzie chewed for a bit and swallowed. "Delicious. I should have had one a long time ago." John smiled and continued eating. He saw Casey working his way over to them.

What the hell does he want? "Is there something you need, Casey?"

Casey frowned and said. "Max is looking for you, John. He needs you to check on Kevin. He has been quiet since he was sent to bed."

John got up. "If you'll excuse me, I better check on him." John started walking toward the trail guide Kevin Johnson's cabin. He heard footsteps behind him but paid no attention.

"John wait up. I need to ask you something." He turned around and saw Mackenzie following him. He stopped and waited for her to catch up.

"Is something wrong, Kenzie?"

Mackenzie blushed, pausing.*Why did he call me that? Nobody has called me that before, not even my own parents.* She continued. "Nothing's wrong. I just didn't want to be near Casey. He creeps me out for some reason."*Usually, I'm used to guys like that hitting on me, but Casey takes it to the next level.* She shuddered at the thought of Casey touching her.

"That's understandable. Casey can be a little bit creepy at times. Some of the female guests that have been here having complained about him trying to get them alone. He has been warned several times. If he ever gets to be too much, find me, Gary and Max. We will straighten him out."

"Thanks, John. I'll make sure to do that. I better leave you to your task. I might go lay down for a bit." Mackenzie waved goodbye to John and went to her cabin. John continued to Kevin's cabin. He knocked on the door, and Kevin answered it.

"Hey, John. Is Casey not leading the trail hike for me?"

He doesn't look sick. In fact, Kevin's dark blue eyes were clear, and his tan skin looked normal. "Are you okay? Casey said that you were sick and couldn't work the trail this afternoon."

Kevin frowned. "Casey came to me and asked if he could take my trail. I told him he could." Kevin's voice trailed off when he saw the look on John's face.

"Thank you for bringing this to my attention. I think it is best if you take over for Casey." John turned on his heel and walked to the main office. He knocked on Max's door.

"Come in." John entered, and Max got up from the desk. "Is something wrong John?"

"I thought that I would bring it to your attention that Casey tried to take Kevin's group without consulting you or me."

Max sighed. "I'll handle it, John. Thank you for telling me." John left with Max behind him. "Why don't you head to the stables and help Dalton get the horses ready for the kids' riding lesson?" John nodded and went to help Dalton.

ackenzie sat on her bed looking over her materials for the Royal Palm Casino advertising deal. She needed to brush up on the material so that she was prepared. She looked at her watch and sighed. *Well, it's time I head for my last lasso lesson.* She left her cabin and headed to the stables for the lesson.

Mackenzie got to the horse corral just as John arrived. They smiled at each other. She saw one of the guests she had made friends with, waving her over.

"Are you ready to practice the lasso?" Tammy Jones laughed when Mackenzie groaned. "That bad, huh?"

"Yes, very much so. I don't think I will ever get the hang of it. Besides, how will it benefit me in my job?" Mackenzie and Tammy laughed. They got quiet as John started the lesson. He showed them a few new moves with the lasso. Then everyone stepped into the corral to practice.

Mackenzie grabbed her lasso and started swinging it like John had shown them. She was startled when she felt someone grab her wrist.

"Here, let me help." John released her wrist and took the lasso from her. "You don't have to hold the rope like you're choking it. Relax your hold a little bit and lightly swing your arm and wrist, Kenzie." Mackenzie blushed at John's nickname for her. She watched as John swung the rope like it was an extension of his arm. She blushed again when he caught her staring.

I shouldn't be having feelings for this man. It would be unprofessional. Besides, it could never work between us. Between the pressures of my job and all the traveling I do, I wouldn't have time to commit to a relationship.

John handed the rope to Mackenzie. "Now it is your turn." He lightly took her wrist and helped her through the motions. "Just like that. Keep your wrist limp and don't choke the rope." He felt a stirring below as he held her wrist.

Her skin is so soft. I wonder what the rest of her feels like. He paused in his musings as he let go of her wrist. He watched her using his advice and getting the hang of swinging the rope. *I can't afford to lose my head over this woman. Besides, if she knew why I 'quit' the rodeo, she wouldn't give me the time of day.*

"Now release the rope." Mackenzie let go of the rope, and it landed right on the horn attached to the hay bale.

"I did it! I can't believe I did it!" Mackenzie threw herself at John and hugged him. He stood there waiting for her to let go but when she didn't, he wrapped his arms around her and hugged back.

They stood there for a bit until someone cleared their throat. Mackenzie broke away and blushed when she saw Gary grinning at them.

"Congrats, Mackenzie. That was mighty fine roping there." Mackenzie blushed even deeper when Gary winked at her. John turned to the others and dismissed them.

"What's up Gary?"

"Supper will be ready in one hour and Max is having us get the south pasture ready for the huge event. The guests are all waiting to go for one more ride before we get started with the bronco riding and barrel racing. Are you going to join, Mackenzie?"

"No thank you. I need to pack. I have to leave in the morning to get to my next meeting in Vegas. I think I know this place better since I've been here. It was a lot of fun."

"Alright. See you at supper and the south pasture for our special event." Gary walked to the stable, leaving the two of them alone.

"I better get packed. See you at supper?" John nodded and Mackenzie walked to her cabin. He walked tothe south pasture to get it ready for the barrel racing and bronco riding.

Mackenzie finished packing and locked up the cabin. She walked to the south pasture and saw Tammy waving her over.

"Why don't you sit with me, Mackenzie? I even brought you a plate of food in case you decide to join me."

Mackenzie smiled at Tammy's thoughtfulness. "Sure I'll sit with you and thanks for the food."

Tammy and Mackenzie walked over to two chairs set up close to the fence of the pasture. Mackenzie gasped at the transformation the pasture had undergone.

It looks like what a rodeo arena might look like. In one area of the pasture was a few barrels set up for the racing. At one end was a gate of some sort where Mackenzie could see a horse fidgeting inside. *I hope that horse is okay. It seems nervous.* Mackenzie started when Max's voice seemed to echo from the middle of the pasture, where he was standing.

"Ladies, gentlemen and children, welcome to our special bronco riding and barrel racing event. We also have a roping contest that we let our guests be a part of. So, I hope everyone is ready. Let's get started." Mackenzie watched as he handed the microphone to John. She gasped when she saw he was clean-shaven.

He looks less rugged that way. He should shave more often.

"Ladies, gentlemen and young ones, are you all excited to see this?" John smiled as he heard the guests cheer. He chuckled at the fact that Mackenzie was louder than the other guests. *Someone is enjoying themselves.* "Our first event is the bronco riding. The first rider is Dalton and the Bronco he is riding is Thunder." John lifted a bullhorn and pressed the trigger.

The gate was released, and the Mustangnamed Thunder rushed out with Dalton on its back. Mackenzie could hear the mustang's hoofs pounding the ground. *I cantell why they call it Thunder. It sounds like a huge thunderstorm.* Mackenzie gasped along with the other guests as Thunder managed to get Dalton off its back. Dalton got off the ground and bowed to the guests as Gary, Casey, and Kevin got the horse out of the pasture.

The bronco riding continued in the same manner. The horses would buck their riders off after a few seconds, and the riders would bow to the guests. After Gary had been bucked off his bronco after only 6 seconds which was longer than any of the other men had been on theirs, Mackenzie waited to hear John announce the next rider and horse. She was surprised to see Max where John had stood.

"Our next rider is used to events like these. Here he is. John on Blaze." Max blew the bullhorn, the gate was released, and John came out of the gate on a beautiful reddish brown stallion. The horse bucked harder than any of the other horses had their riders. Mackenzie held her breath as John held on tight to the horse.

After 30 secondshad passed, the stallion slowed down and finally stopped. John was still on Blaze. Mackenzie released her breath and cheered along with the other guests. John hopped off Blaze and bowed deeply to the crowd. He came back up and saw Mackenzie smiling and clapping.

He smiled and led Blaze away from the pasture.*I wish the owners of the rodeo could have seen me now. That was my best time ever.* He grinned and handed Blaze's reins to Gary. Gary clapped John on the shoulder and led Blaze back to the stables as Max announced the barrel race would begin in two minutes. Dalton handed John Blackjack's reins.

"Ready for me to beat you at this?" John slapped Dalton's back. Dalton grinned.

"You willing to make a bet on that?" John shook his head and led Blackjack to the pasture.

The barrel race was the best part of the event. Mackenzie enjoyed watching John race around the barrels without so much as brushing them. Gary won second place while John won first place. When the sun set and Max had some big lights brought out to illuminate the pasture, Mackenzie turned to Tammy and told her that she was going to bed. Tammy nodded and bid Mackenzie good night. Mackenzie walked toward her cabin.

Halfway there, Mackenzie turned around when she heard John call to her. She watched as he hurried over.

"I saw you leave and thought you might need help getting to your cabin in the dark."

Mackenzie smiled and grabbed onto John's proffered arm. They walked to her cabin in silence. Mackenzie couldn't believe that she had to leave in the morning. Mackenzie sighed. *And here I was finally enjoying it here. I'll miss this.*

John walked Mackenzie to the door of her cabin and waited to make sure she got in safely. He was stunned when she turned toward him.

"I liked watching you ride. Makes me wish I didn't have to leave."

"I'm glad you liked it tonight. I'll let you get some sleep." John started walking off as Mackenzie unlocked the door.

"John?"

John turned back when he heard Mackenzie call his name.

Mackenzie stood in the doorway, not wanting to go inside. John rushed over to her, leaned forward and kissed her. She closed her eyes and wrapped her arms around his neck. The kiss was everything she had imagined it would be-sweet, gentle, but yet filled with passion and the desire for more. He slid his hands up her back, caressing her hair and cupping her head as he deepened the kiss. His tongue slipped into her mouth-soft, but certain- and she responded in kind, flicking the tip of her tongue against his own. He lifted her up, pressing her body against his, and guided her over to the bed. He lay her down slowly, carefully, and stood for a moment above her as he took in her body beneath him. Her skin was flawless, and John was unable to resist the urge to reach down and skim his fingers across her cheek- her eyes drifted shut, and she let out the softest moan. John could already feel himself growing hard, and quickly pulled off his shirt and climbed on top of her, kissing her with more ferocity than he ever thought he had in him.

She raised her hips to meet him, skimming her fingers over his bare back and enjoying the feeling of his strength beneath her hands. His tongue was immediate and hungry this time, his hands pushing up her shirt and grabbing at her waist as he ground against her. Mackenzie pulled back for a moment, taking in his expression as his erection pressed hard and needy against her groin- his eyes were flashing with desire, his breath coming in short bursts as he stared back at her. He leaned down and kissed her neck, his mouth warm and soft against her skin, and she gripped his hair as he began to work his way down, towards her breasts.

He pulled down the top of her shirt, exposing her chest, and slipped a hand beneath the cup of her bra, pinching her nipple between his thumb and forefinger. He glanced up at her, a small smile on his face, as her mouth fell open slightly and her brow tensed. It felt good- she could already feel the sensation spreading down towards her pussy, her body already aching for him.

John tugged her shirt over her head in one smooth motion, and continued down her torso and towards the top of her pants. He hooked his fingers round her beltloops, and slowly inched them down till she was naked but for her bra and panties. She couldn't take her eyes off him-focusing on the look on his face, the feeling of his fingers against her skin. He leaned down, and pressed a kiss on the outside of her panties, sending shockwaves of pleasure through her body. Her mouth dropped open again, and this time she knew what she wanted- she needed him, his mouth on her, and he seemed to understand the pressing nature of her desire. He slowly inched her panties down her hips and slipped between her legs, casting another look up at her as he hovered his mouth just above her aching pussy. And then, he leaned down and sealed his lips around her.

Mackenzie had never been one for being particularly loud during sex, but she couldn't hold back the groan that forced it's way from between her lips as his tongue went to work on her clit. He started by flicking the very tip gently against her, as if testing her out, before he began to suck lightly on her pussy and move his tongue in long, slow motions against her clit. With one hand, he grabbed her ass and pulled her further on to him, and with the other, he slid two fingers slowly into her slit, fucking her with his hand at a langorous pace as he hungrily ate her out. She shut her eyes-this was too much. She could already feel her body tensing, the orgasm threatening as he moved his fingers in and out of her, matching them to the pace of his tongue-then suddenly, he stopped.

"Huh?" Mackenzie raised her head.

"I really want to fuck you right now," he replied, his voice ragged, as he grabbed a condom from his pocket and quickly undressed. Mackenzie stared up at him, teetering on the very brink of an orgasm, and knew then that she didn't care how she got there- she just wanted to come.

"Do it," she murmured, as he sheathed himself quickly and positioned his cock at the entrance to her pussy. She draped a leg over his shoulder, and John slowly eased himself inside her till his full seven inches were buried in her cunt.

"Fuck," he gasped, as he began to fuck her slowly. Mackenzie let her eyes roll back as he screwed her- he felt perfect, just enough, and she was already so turned-on that her natural lubrication made things so much slicker. He grabbed her hips with one hand, and used the thumb of the other to gently stimulate her clit as he began to pick up his pace. She stared up at him- so close, but so far away- as he towered above her, his eyes lost to the pleasure of their sex.

And then, suddenly, it hit her- the orgasm tore through

her body like wildfire, the heat burning through her and making all her muscles tense at once. She cried out, her head tilting back as she allowed the waves of pleasure to course through her, her pussy grasping at his dick as she came. Seeing her in the throes of pleasure like that was enough to tip John over the edge, and he came a few moments later, his head bowed and his teeth gritted. He slowly pulled out of her, and lay his head down on the pillow beside her.

"Good?" He murmured, tracing her cheekbone with his finger, and she nodded, still unable to speak.

"Good," he smiled, and leaned over to plant a kiss on her collarbone. The night was far from over yet.

CHAPTER 5

John woke up with the sun shining on his face. He looked at his watch and saw that he had slept too long. *Oh shit, did I forget to set the alarm on my watch?*He looked down and saw Mackenzie in his arms. Mackenzie opened her eyes when John left the bed.

"John, what time is it?" Mackenzie looked at her phone and paled. *I'm late! I need to hurry.* Mackenzie hopped out of bed and rushed to take a fast shower. While she was in the shower, John got dressed and snuck out of her cabin, making sure none of the guests were out. He saw Casey exit one of the other cabins but dismissed it.

Mackenzie got out of the shower and found a box on the bed. She dressed quickly and picked up the box. She opened it and smiled at the note and gift John left for her.

John watched Mackenzie's car drove off toward Vegas. He smiled when he saw that she was wearing the hairpin he had bought her from the gift shop.

He walked toward the stables to get the corral set up for the kids' lasso lesson. When he got there, he saw Gary glaring at Casey. Casey was yelling about something, but John couldn't catch what he was yelling about.

"What the hell is going on here?" Both men looked toward John surprised to find him there. Casey was the first to recover.

"You dare to ask that after what you did last night! You have had far too much leeway around here. You don't belong here. You have had it out for me since day one. I am the only one you seem to have a problem with. If the gay guy does something against the rules, Heavenforbids if you so much as punish him."

"Hey, at least I don't try and pursue the single women who come here to relax and learnwhat it is like to live on a ranch." Gary sneered at Casey, who paled.

"This doesn't concern you, homo." Gary surprised John and Casey by grabbing Casey by his shirt.

"When are you going to realize that I consider myself to be John's friend and therefore what you say about him does concern me, you got that asshole?" Gary dropped Casey and walked off. John took one look at Casey and followed Gary.

Casey got up and headed to the main office. *I will teach that bastard to mess with me.*

After John had got Gary calmed down, he went back to the corral. He found Dalton standing by the corral with a frown on his face.

"What's going on, Dalton?"

Dalton sighed. "Max wants to see you in his office. He looks mad enough to spit nails."

John frowned. "Do you know what he is mad about?"

"All I know is Casey went into Max's office, and now Max is really pissed off. So you might want to get there asap before he gets even more pissed off." John ran to the main office and knocked on Max's door.

"Come in." John entered, and Max scowled at him. He noticed Casey standing in the corner, grinning at him.

"What happened?"

"As if you didn't know. I have trusted you to help me run this place. Casey has brought it to my attention that you acted in an unprofessional manner."

Casey grinned and stepped forward. "Just this morning, he threatened me when I was having a little argument with Gary over who would run the gift shop this afternoon."

John opened his mouth toprotest, but Max glared at him.

"He has accused me several times of sleeping with a few of the guests here. That is simply not true. However, I know for a fact that he has slept with Miss Tucker, who was a guesthere if I am not mistaken." Max paled at Casey's accusation.

"John, did you sleep with Miss Tucker while she was here?"

"I am not going to deny it,however; I will say that Gary and Casey were not fighting about who would run the gift shop. In fact, Casey was talking trash about me, and Gary was just defending me."

Max sighed. "I'm sorry John, but you broke our number one rule. You slept with a guest. I am going to have to fire you. I'm sorry." John paled.

"Max, I need this job. My grandpa's ranch…"

Max shook his head. "I want you to grab your things and leave, John. I'm sorry it had to be this way, but you knew the rule." John left the room, but before the door closed behind him, he saw Casey grin at him and wave goodbye.

John walked to his cabin feeling as if his world had ended. He couldn't believe what Casey had done. *How did he know I had slept with her?* Then John remembered seeing Casey by the guest cabins just that morning as he was leaving Mackenzie's cabin. *That bastard! He was probably there sleeping with one of the guests.* John was about to turn back to the main office when he saw Max watching him. He sighed and continued to his cabin.

He entered his cabin and looked around. He had considered this place to be his home, and now he had nowhere to go. He sighed and started packing what little belongings he had.

Mackenzie entered the casino and was directed to the head office. She straightened her suit and walked into the office.

"Aw, Miss Tucker. So glad you could make it. I have been looking forward to this meeting for a while. Please, won't you sit?" The casino owner smiled at her and gestured to the chair in front of the desk.

"Thank you, Mr. Rosen." Mackenzie sat down and pulled out her ideas for the casino advertising campaign. When she sat back up, she noticed the owner frowning at her. "Here are the ideas I had on what we can do for your advertising campaign." She handed the owner her proposal. He flipped through the pages and handed it back to her.

"I'm sorry, Miss Tucker but I cannot have someone who shows up in an unprofessional manner representing my casino."

Mackenzie frowned. "I'm sorry, Mr. Rosen but what do you mean?"

"I arranged this meeting because I was told that you always act in a professional manner. However, you arrived late. To top it off, you come in here wearing a very gaudy piece of jewelry in your hair. So, therefore, I will not be a client now or anytime in the future. I have decided to go withShiyoto Media instead." The owner got up and pointed to the door. "I have to ask you to leave." Mackenzie got up and glared at him.

"I'm sorry you feel that way, Mr. Rosen. Thank you for meeting me. Have a good day sir." She pushed past the owner and left the room. She left the casino with her head held high. She got into her car and drove back to the ranch with a smile. *The deal may have fallen through, but at least I can visit John.* She grinned, remembering the note he had written her.

Sorry, I had to leave.

**Here is a little gift for you
A lasso to celebrate your first successful roping challenge.
Truly yours, John**

She lifted her face to the sun and drove back to the ranch with a happy feeling in her heart. *Won't John be surprised to see me? I might stay for a bit more this time. I might even ask my boss for a little vacation time. Lord knows I need it.* Mackenzie smiled and drove a bit faster.

Mackenzie parked beside Max's truck and walked to his office.

"Wait up, Mackenzie. I need to talk to you a minute." Mackenzie turned and saw Gary running up to her.

"Hey, Gary. Is something wrong?" The instant she asked, she regretted it. Gary was frowning, and his skin was pale.

"Max fired John." Her heart dropped when she heard the hurt in Gary's voice.

"What happened?"

"Casey accused John of threatening him and then said that he slept with you. Is it true, the sleeping with you part at least?"

Mackenzie paled and then felt angry. "Let me straighten this out Gary. Thank you for telling me." Mackenzie stomped off to the office. She entered the office after knocking on the door.

Max jumped up and went to shake her hand. When she didn't return the handshake, he dropped his hand to his side. "What can I do for you, Miss Tucker?"

"Is it true that you fired John?"

"Yes, I did. He broke our number one rule here."

"And what rule would that be, if you don't mind me asking?"

Max was startled at the anger in her voice. "He slept with a guest. He also threatened one of the men who works here. We cannot have someone here who could get us sued. I'm sorry, Miss Tucker, but I had to let him go."

"Is there any way to get his job back?"

"I'm sorry Miss Tucker. You were a guest here, and he broke the rule."

Mackenzie felt as if her face was on fire. "He never forced himself on me, and I allowed it to happen. I want you to give him his job back, now!"

Max frowned. "I am going to have to ask you to leave. I will inform your boss that I am canceling our contract. Have a good day, Miss Tucker."

Mackenzie turned on her heel and stomped out of the building. She almost was to her car when she heard shouting over by the stables. She rushed over as fast as she could in her heels and saw the stable hand, Dalton holding Casey back.

"Next time you decide to cause trouble here, no one will bail you out. You're an asshole and don't deserve to work here." Gary advanced on Dalton and Casey. "Dalton let him go if you don't want to get your ass kicked too." Dalton let go of him and stepped back. Casey straightened his clothes and grinned.

"Bring it on, you bastard. Serves John right. Besides, once a drunkard always a drunkard."

Gary yelled and tackled Casey to the ground. Gary held him down and started punching him. Mackenzie rushed over, but Dalton held her back.

"Let me go. He may deserve it, but Gary will kill him. I have to stop him."

"There is nothing you can do, Miss Tucker. At least with

this. Someone needs to stop John from making a fool of himself. He is at the bar in town."

"But…"

"Go Miss Tucker. I will stop Gary. Go!" Dalton released Mackenzie, and she ran to her car. She fumbled with the keys but managed to get the car started. She rushed out of the space and sped down the highway as fast as the speed limit allowed. Her vision blurred, and she blinked to clear it.

How could that creep do that?I hope Gary kills him. He deserves it for what he did to John. Her vision blurred again, and she blinked to clear her vision. Then she realized that she was crying. *Why am I crying? I just met John, but I already love him.* She pulled over to the side of the road. *I can't believe I thought that. I have never had a serious relationship before and the first man I find myself even remotely drawn to, I get him fired and discover that I love him.* She wiped her eyes and sighed. *I really love him, and I need to find him to tell him so.* Mackenzie pulled back onto the highway and continued to town.

John sat at the bar, staring at the glass of whiskey in his hands. He couldn't believe that he was about to go back on the drink. *Have I come full circle to what started my troubles to begin with?* He sighed. The night before kept running through his head. The night he even felt like his life was on the right track. *It was bound to happen anyway. I deserved to be fired just like I deserve to get drunk.* He is about to finally take the drink that would change his life for the worst when someone sat beside him.

"Hey cowboy, would you like some company?"

John glanced up in surprise at seeing Mackenzie sitting beside him. "Miss Tucker, what are you doing here? Shouldn't you be in Vegas making an advertising deal?"

"I was, but the deal fell through.Besides, I told you to call me Mackenzie."

"Why are you here?"

Mackenzie turned to him. "I came back to see you, but I was told you were fired. I tried to get your job back, but it didn't work out.

"Listen to me. You cannot afford to get drunk. There are people who care about you back at the ranch. In fact, Gary beat the crap out of Casey for what he did to you. The stable hand Dalton even told me where you were."

"I'm sorry. I should not have done that last night. I…"

Mackenzie placed a finger on his lips. "Never apologize for last night. It was wonderful and don't think I regret it for one minute. John, I love you, and I do not care if anyone knows it. I may lose my job, but I don't want to lose you." Her lips replaced her finger. He raised his hand and took out the hairpin and released her hair from the bun. He then ran his fingers through her hair.

John pulled away and smiled. "I love you too, Kenzie. So now what happens?"

"Well, first we need to leave this bar. This place is too dark." John laughed and helped her off the bar stool. They left and went to her car.

"I'm parked over there. I'm staying at a motel at the moment until I can find a place to live. You're welcome to come by."

"I would like that." He turned to walk to his car when she said, "John if you want I can help you keep your grandfather's ranch."

John turned toward her and smiled. "Thank you, Kenzie. I would like that." He grabbed her and kissed her with everything in him. "I love you, Mackenzie Tucker, and don't you think I regret last night either." He left her to let his words sink in.

Mackenzie followed John to where he was staying. He got out of his truck and went to open her door. He helped her get out and went to unlock his motel room. He picked her up and carried her inside, kissing her as if it would be the last. He laid her on the bed and kissed her.

"John, I love you so much."

He smiled. "I know, Kenzie." He leaned down and kissed her long and hard. "I know."

CHAPTER 6

Mackenzie looked up at her condo in Chicago. She looked over and saw John staring in awe at the red stucco.

"So, what do you think, honey? Welcome home." Mackenzie walked over and hugged him.

"It's big; I'll give you that," John smiled down at her and kissed the top of her head. "I will tell you though as long as I'm with you, any place is home." She smiled and unlocked the door.

"It's Monday, so we have the house to ourselves. Let me give you a tour of the place." Mackenzie led John to the kitchen. "Would you like some coffee? I think I remember where Natalie keeps the coffee."

"Natalie?"

"Natalie is my housekeeper. Monday is her day off."

John looked around and sighed. He still couldn't believe he had found someone who loved him like Mackenzie did. He was even more surprised when she asked him to come to Chicago with her.

"Earth to John. How do you like your coffee?"

"Sorry, love. I wasn't paying attention."

Mackenzie smiled. "I knew that. I asked how you drink your coffee."

"Black," John smiled and took the cup of coffee from Mackenzie. He took a sip and placed the cup on the counter. He picked her up and started walking. "Which way to the bedroom?"

Mackenzie giggled and pointed down the hall. "First room on the right." He walked in the direction of where she pointed. He walked into the room and placed her on the bed. He was about to climb onto the bed when the doorbell rang.

Mackenzie sat up. "Who could that be? Wait here." She got off the bed and John grabbed her arm.

He pulled her to him and whispered, "Maybe if we're quiet, they'll go away." He kissed her and she giggled as the doorbell rang again.

"I need to answer that. It could be important." John groaned when she pulled away. She left the room and went to see who was at the door.

She looked out the peephole and saw her neighbor

standing on the small porch. "Hi, Christina. Is something wrong?"

Christina Banes took off her sunglasses and smiled. Christina had her curly blonde hair back in a perfect up do. Her hazel eyes were bright and clear. "Hey, Mackenzie. I saw your car and came over to see how you were doing. I was wondering if you knew who's truck that was blocking my driveway?"

"Oh sorry, Christina. I will ask them to move it when I see them." Mackenzie was about to close the door when Christina put her foot up to stop it.

"You don't mind if I come in, do you? I want to catch up." Before Mackenzie could reply, she walked in the house.

Mackenzie watched as Christina looked around. "Actually, now is not the best time Christina. I mean I just got back and wanted to rest for a bit."

Christina picked up the cup that John had used and placed it back on the counter. She turned to Mackenzie and smiled.

"So who is he?"

"I have no clue who you mean."

"Come on, Mackenzie. You know exactly what I'm talking about. I saw him in your yard. So, who is he?"

Just then John walked in the room. Christina looked him up and down and then scrunched her nose as if she smelled something horrible. Mackenzie frowned. John went over and kissed Mackenzie's head.

"Pleased to meet you, ma'am. I'm John Daniels." He held out his hand, and Christina shook it once and wiped her hand off on her slacks.

"John, honey, this is my next door neighbor Christina Banes. Your truck is blocking her driveway. Could you moveit, please? You can park it next to my car." John nodded and went outside.

Mackenzie waited until he was out of earshot when she turned to Christina. "That was very rude, Christina. He is a guest in my home, and I don't appreciate you acting like John is some insect."

"I'm sorry, Mackenzie. I never thought you went with the rugged type. I could have set you up with Tom's cousin."

"I do not need help finding a date. I love John and if you don't like him then just say so." She was about to continue her rant when John entered.

"There you go, ma'am. I'm sorry to have blocked your drive."

Christina smiled. "Thank you so much, Mr. Daniels. It was nice meeting you." She turned to leave and then turned back to Mackenzie. "I'm glad you made it back, Mackenzie. I'll talk to you later."

Once she left, Mackenzie let out a sigh of relief. John came over and wrapped her in his arms.

"Are you okay?" Mackenzie nodded. "She seemed a little...."

"Uppity. That is the word you are looking for."

He smiled. "I was going to say nosy but uppity works." They burst into laughter.

Once they caught their breath, John reached over and hugged Mackenzie. "How about we finish what we started before anyone else comes by to be nosy?"

"Sounds like a plan to me." He picked her up again and carried her to the bedroom.

Mackenzie woke up the next morning with John holding her. She tried to wiggle away to get ready to go to work.

"Please stop moving. I don't think I will be able to let you go if you keep wiggling." Mackenzie giggled and wiggled some more. John groaned and flipped her on her back. "I warned you. Now you can't escape me." He smiled, and she kissed him. He let her go running his fingers through her hair. She took advantage of his momentary distraction and got off the bed.

"I really need to get to work, John. I need to know if I still have a job or not." He groaned and rolled back over in bed.

"I was looking forward to seeing the city with you today."

She walked into the bathroom and started the shower. "I was looking forward to that today too. Sadly, I can't get away. I have an idea. Why don't you explore the house and get a feel for it? Natalie will be in at noon so you will have the house to yourself until then." John groaned in response and Mackenzie laughed. She hopped in the shower and let the warm water rush over her.

Mackenzie was gone when John woke up about an hour later. He got up and took a quick shower and then went into the kitchen for a cup of coffee. He entered the kitchen and was getting a cup from the cabinet when he heard a scream.

He looked toward the source of the scream and saw a red haired woman in uniform brandishing a broom. "Hold on, ma'am. I'm not a burglar. I'm Mackenzie's guest. I guess she didn't tell you that she was back and had a guest." The woman screamed again and hit him with the broom.

"How did you get in here? I will call the police. How do you know Miss Mackenzie?"

"Ma'am, I will tell you if you quit hitting me and screaming." The woman stopped hitting him and put her hands on her hips.

"You have one minute to explain what you are doing here, or I'm calling the police."

John nodded. "My name is John Daniels. Mackenzie invited me here with her. We met while she was working. I worked at the dude ranch where she was helping advertise the place on the radio."

He launched into the rest of his story while the woman listened. By the end of it, she had calmed down and laughed with him when he told her about Mackenzie's horrible attempts to use the lasso.

"I'm sorry I hit you with the broom. I didn't know who it was that was in the shower. I thought someone had broken in."

"It is alright, ma'am. I would have done the same thing if I had been the one in your place."

"Please call me Natalie. I'm Miss Mackenzie's housekeeper."

John smiled. "Mackenzie told me about you, but she told me you wouldn't be here until noon."

Natalie Mitchell shook her head. "She forgets I come in around ten on Tuesday. I only come in at noon the rest of the week. I swear that girl runs around like she has a fire lit under her butt." John laughed.

"I know what you mean. While she was at the ranch, she was always running here and there like a chicken with her head cut off. She was either doing something with Gary, who is one of the trail guides and then the next minute she was trying to get away from Casey, who is one of the other trail guides. However, I think she had fun while she was there. I especially liked having her company. Sometimes we would take the horses and go riding together. Sometimes Gary would come with us."

Natalie smiled. "At least she had fun. When she is in the city, she stays busy. Mostly she travels. I know it is hard onher, but she doesn't complain." She looked at the clock and went into the kitchen. "Would you like something to eat Mr. Daniels?"

"Please call me John and yes I would like something to eat if you don't mind."

Mackenzie waited in the reception area of her boss' office. *It is sure taking him a long time to see me. It must be bad.* She fiddled with the hem of her skirt. She was startled when the receptionist Chelsea Connors touched her shoulder.

"Miss Tucker, he will see you now."

"Thank you, Chelsea." She got up and walked into the office. "You wished to see me, sir?"

Her boss Jacob Masters looked up from the paperwork. His brown hair with gray streaks in it was smoothed back with hair gel, and there was a rumor going around that his blue eyes could make any woman want to sleep with him. Mackenzie never put much stock in that rumor.

"Yes, I did. Please sit." Mackenzie sat down and fiddled with the hem of her skirt again. Her boss wrote a few more things down before folding his hands on the desk.

"I called you in here to go over what happened in

Nevada. You not only lost us the casino deal but you also cost us the ranch deal. Now, what do you have to say about that?"

Mackenzie sat in silence before answering. "Sir, I know I acted out of line."

"You acted in an unprofessional manner. I'm sorry, but I have to let you go. Gather your things from your desk, Miss Tucker."

Mackenzie got up and exited the office. She headed to her desk, gathered her stuff, which wasn't much, and got in her car. She drove around a bit before heading home. *I hope John's day was better than mine.*

Natalie went to the store around noon. John decided to mow the lawn to surprise Mackenzie. He got out the push mower and started mowing. He waved to Christina next door,and she rushed inside. *That was rude. Oh well.*

He just started on the back lawn when a man in a dark Armani suit came up. He paused in his mowing to talk to him.

"Can I help you, sir?" The man stared at him and then looked at the lawn.

"Yes, you can. I don't know if Miss Tucker told you, but here in this neighborhood, we have set rules on how to maintain our homes." The man frowned and took out a measuring tape. He measured the height of the grass and frowned again. "This grass is too short."

John stared at the man in disbelief. "What do you mean it is too short?"

"Exactly like I said. You have mowed this grass too short. I will have to report this to the Committee. Miss Tucker will receive a warning through the mail. Good day, sir."

John grabbed the man by the shirt and looked him in the eyes. "Look here, I was doing this as a surprise. I can tell that the grass is the right height." The man paled.

"I'm sorry, but we have set rules..." He trailed off when John pulled him a little closer.

"I won't say this again. The grass is just fine. I have been mowing since I was six, so I know a thing or two about mowing grass." He released the man, who took off in a run. John sighed and put the lawn mower away. He went inside, took a shower and sat in the living room area. He didn't say anything when Natalie came back. He dozed off in the armchair while waiting for Mackenzie to get home.

Mackenzie got home and saw that Natalie's car was in the drive. *I forgot to warn Natalie about John.* She rushed inside and found John asleep in the armchairby the window. *He must have had a good day. He has fallen asleep.*

Mackenzie walked into the bedroom and found Natalie putting clothes away. "I'm home early, Natalie. You can take the rest of the day off."

Natalie jumped in surprise. "Miss Mackenzie, you startled me."

"I'm sorry Natalie. I had a long morning. I hope John didn't scare you. I forgot to tell you about him."

"That's okay, Miss Mackenzie. I admit I did hit him with the broom." They both giggled as the phone rang. "I'll get that Miss Mackenzie." Natalie left the room to pick up the phone.

Mackenzie sighed and changed into her non-work clothes. She felt John slide his hands down her arms.

"I missed you, city girl." Mackenzie laughed, turned around and kissed him.

"Back at you, cowboy." She ran her hands through his slightly damp hair. She moaned into his mouth as he caressed her back. They broke apart when Natalie cleared her throat.

"Miss Mackenzie, Miss Garrett is on the phone."

"Thank you, Natalie. I'll take it into the living room." She turned to John. "I'll be back. Why don't you get ready and we will go out to dinner? This time my treat." John smiled and kissed her.

"Sounds like a plan."

Mackenzie left him to get ready. She was looking forward to showing him the city at night. *I think I will take us to Enzo's. We won't need a reservation. After all, I did help him advertise his restaurant.*

Mackenzie came back to the bedroom after getting off the phone and seeing Natalie to her car to find John partially dressed. She admired his bareback for a while. He caught her staring and grabbed her in his arms.

"What was that about?"

"Looks like we aren't going out to eat. In fact, we were invited to dinner at one of my friend's house."

"Sounds good to me. Is there anything special I need to wear?"

"Just wear something clean. I'll be wearing something special." Mackenzie smiled at the look in John's eyes. *That got him interested. I just hope Macy likes him. Actually, come to think about it, she might not.* Mackenzie sighed, and John held her.

"Let's hope tonight is a success, Kenzie love." He kissed her one more time and put on a clean shirt. He left the room so that she could change without him bugging her.

Mackenzie picked out a dark red dress and dark red wedge heels that her personal shopper Janine Barnett had picked out for her. According to Janine, a similar dress was worn by Reese Witherspoon to an award show. With all the traveling, Mackenzie never got to wear it, however.

I hope John likes it. Mackenzie hopped in the shower for a quick shower before getting dressed.

The instant John entered Mackenzie's friend's house; he knew he was out of place. Mackenzie squeezed his hand.

"I'm right here. You have nothing to worry about honey." Mackenzie tried not to show how nervous she was. *I hope that she likes him. This isthe first time I have been in a serious relationship.* She sighed and smiled as Macy Garrett walked up to them. She had her strawberry-blond pulled back with a jeweled clip, her hazel eyes shining in her excitement.

"Mackenzie, I'm so glad you could make it. This must be John!" Macy held her hand out for John to shake. He returned the handshake and Macy smiled. "My, you have a nice warm handshake. Mackenzie, don't ever give this man up." Mackenzie was surprised to how well Macy seemed to accept John.

"I don't plan on it. I like what you did to the place."

"Thanks, Mackenzie. You know since Calvin died, I have been trying to figure out how I would redecorate. I finally decided to go with an Egyptian décor."

"Well, I think it makes the room look brighter," Macy smiled and led them to the dining room. *Looks like she invited everyone.* Cassandra Mathews, her blond hair piled on top of her head and green eyes sparkling was talking to Christina, who had her blonde hair loose around her shoulders, about the new gardener that her husband hired. Beside them was Tamera Jones, who was said to turn the heads of any man within a ten-mile radius, sipping a martini. With her brown eyes and dark brown hair, she could have graced the pages of Vogue. Sitting next to her was Theresa Evens, who was tapping on her phone. Her husband worked for the biggest law firm in Chicago.

"Mackenzie's here with her date. Now the party can begin." The other woman glanced up and smiled at Mackenzie. All the women except for Macy and Christina, who were chatting, looked from her and stared at John like he was some sort of freak. Mackenzie blushed. *Why are they staring at him like that?*She looked to John to see if he saw their reaction to him. He looked down and raised her hand to his lips and kissed it.

"Aw, that was sweet! Calvin used to do the same thing." Macy smiled sadly but recovered fast. "Why don't we all sit-down and catch up? With all our schedules conflicting, it is hard for all of us to get together like this." Mackenzie and John sat closest to Macy. Macy rang a bell, and a servant offered Mackenzie and John water or martinis. They both took a bottle of water. Cassandra raised an eyebrow.

"What's wrong Mackenzie? Usually, you drink martinis with us. Perhaps since you have a boyfriend, you think you're better than us." Mackenzie paled. Cassandra laughed and said, "I was only kidding."

I can't believe she said that. The only reason I'm friends with her is thatshe is married to Macy's brother . The other women seemed to take Cassandra's comment to be a joke.

John could tell that the so-called joke hurt Mackenzie.

He squeezed her hand under the table.

"So tell us how the two of you met?" Macy seemed interested.

"It isn't that interesting. I was at a dude ranch and met him while helping to get the ranch and others like it advertising."

The other woman looked startled. "Weren't you scared of snakes and things?" Theresa asked.

"I didn't see any snakes. It was really nice out there. I rode horses and learned to use a lasso. In fact, John had bought me a hairpin in the shape of a lasso, see?" Mackenzie turned her head to the side so they could see it.

"It is pretty, Mackenzie. That was sweet of him." Macy smiled.

"Thanks, Macy," John smiled at the pride in Mackenzie's voice. *At least they like it. It was all I could find that I thought Kenzie would like.*

The servant came back with the plates of food. Everyone ate in silence. Occasionally, Macy would ask a question to John, and he would reply. After eating, John asked where the bathroom was.

"I'll show you. It's this way." John followed Macy to the bathroom.

The instant they were out of earshot, the woman started laughing.

"Did you hear how he talked? It was hilarious!" Theresa giggled.

"I know. Where did you pick him up from? The backcountry?" Tamera laughed. Mackenzie could feel her face become hot with embarrassment.

Cassandra grinned. "Is that all he could afford? That hairpin is so garish."

"Well, Mackenzie. I swear you could do better than country bumpkin there." Christina took a sip of her drink while the others laughed.

Mackenzie got up from her chair and slapped the table. The women got quiet. "How dare you talk about him like that! So what if he isn't sophisticated. I love him, and if you can't be happy for me then all of you can go to hell!" Mackenzie left them in silence. She passed by Macy as she was coming into the room.

"Mackenzie, what's wrong?" Mackenzie continued walking down the hallway. She found John as he was on his way back to the dining room. She grabbed his arm and drug him to the front door.

"Kenzie, what happened?" He saw tears running down her face.

"I don't want to talk about it. I just want to go home." They left the house and went to his truck. He helped her in and got in on the driver's side. He looked over at her and saw her take the hair pin out. She put it in her purse and wiped her eyes.

They drove home in silence. Once they were inside, Mackenzie went into the bedroom while John fixed her some hot chocolate. He remembered Natalie telling him that hot chocolate was Mackenzie's comfort drink. He brought it into Mackenzie but saw she fell asleep. He sighed. He placed the drink on the nightstand. He got undressed and climbed into bed. He gathered Mackenzie close to him and held her. He felt her snuggle closer to him, and he fell asleep.

The rest of the week did not fare so well. Mackenzie had trouble finding another job. She refused to take her friends' calls. She was short with Natalie and John whenever they asked how the job search was going.

John didn't do so well that week either. He had two more run-ins with someone from the neighborhood committee. One of the incidents ended in John yelling at the committee member. The man threatened to call the police. John knew that if he were arrested, Mackenzie would be upset. To top it off, he was having trouble adjusting to the noise of cars honking and sirens going off every few minutes. He missed hearing crickets and seeing the stars at night. He never complained, though.

One night, Mackenzie came home in a bad mood. She spent the day going from one radio advertising agency to another to get a job. At each one, she was turned away.

Macy called her on her cell phone and Mackenzie yelled at her. She felt bad about later but didn't call Macy back to apologize.

Mackenzie found John sitting in the armchair by the window. He turned to her and smiled sadly.

"Kenzie, we need to talk." Mackenzie paled. *This isit. We are breaking up. I was so mean to him and Natalie this week.* Mackenzie could almost see him walking out the door and never seeing him again.

John patted the arm of the chair, and Mackenzie sat down. He wrapped his arm around her waist. "I know this week has been hard on you. I want to let you know that I am here for you. I want you to be happy."

"John I love you, but I'm not sure it is working out. I think we should..."

"No need to say anymore. I am not happy here, and neither are you. In fact, living in the city makes my head hurt. I'm used to hearing crickets and frogs at night, not honking horns and sirens every few minutes. I can't do any yard work without being yelled at by the neighborhood association. I've had a few arguments with some of the members." Mackenzie laughed at the look on John's face.

"John, I know I was short with you all week. I need to tell you about what happened the night we went to Macy's. While you were in the bathroom and Macy wasn't in the room, they started in on you. They said some really hateful things, and I couldn't sit there and let them do that. I told them to go to hell." John sat there for a bit, letting her words sink in.

He cleared his throat. "That was sweet of you to tell them off. No wonder when they would call, you didn't answer. Baby, you know you can always tell me when something is wrong. I love you Mackenzie Tucker, and I will never stop loving you."

Mackenzie's eyes filled with tears and she kissed him. "I think we should move to New Mexico and fix your grandfather's ranch like we talked about. It will be good for us. I don't think I am cut out to be a cog in the corporate machine. I think we can get the ranch up and running."

"Kenzie, I would love that. I think we should give it a go." John smiled, picked her up and carried her to the bedroom to celebrate their decision.

CHAPTER 7

"Damn it all to hell!" Mackenzie started when John yelled.

"John, honey, are you sure you don't want me to call a plumber?"

John crawled out of the crawl space covered in dirt. "I can get it Kenzie. If my grandfather could fix the pipes without calling a plumber, I can as well."

Mackenzie sighed and went inside the house. She still couldn't believe that she was here. When they arrived a month ago, the house was a mess. They finally managed to get the house cleaned but ran into the problem of no running water or electricity. Now John was working on getting the water and plumbing ready. She was worried that when he started on the wiring in the house, he would shock himself even though there was no electricity running.

John entered the house and went straight to the cooler they had bought. He opened it and pulled out a bottle of water.

"I think I will take a break on the plumbing and get started on fixing the barn.

"Sounds good. I'll get started on dinner." Mackenzie was glad that the stove worked. They were able to pay for the gas to be turned back on. *Now all we need is electricity and running water; thenwe will be set .* John kissed her and went outside to get started on the barn.

Mackenzie watched him walk to the barn . *I wish he will just admit it and hire an electrician and plumber. I know I am asking a lot of him,but damn, a girl needs a hot shower and a way to plug in a blow dryer.* She sighed and opened the cooler. She pulled out a bag of vegetables and package of hamburger. She went to one of the cupboards and pulled out a pan and skillet that they had bought before moving there. She turned on the stove and lit the pilot. Once it lit, she placed the skillet on the burner and put the meat in it. She lit the burner and put the pot on it. She took the medium sized water jug and poured some water into the pot. She then opened the bag of vegetables and poured them into the pot. Mackenzie smiled to herself. She remembered Natalie teaching her how to use a stove.

Two weeks before her and John were to leave the condo, she turned to Natalie one afternoon.

"Natalie, could you teach me to cook?"

Natalie looked startled. "Miss Mackenzie, I don't think I could teach you to cook. It's not that I won't teach you, it's that you are leaving here and going to a new place. Are you even sure it has a stove?"

"I asked John, and he said he remembered his grandfather having a gas one. That is why I'm asking if you could teach me to cook."

Natalie smiled. "I'm sure I could teach you. However, the stove here uses electricity to cook."

"That's fine as long as I will be able to cook for John," Natalie smiled and showed Mackenzie how to turn on the stove and explained how to turn on a gas stove. She told her that she wouldn't need to light the oven part of the stove, that it would automatically light itself. Natalie taught her all that she could those two weeks.

Mackenzie broke away from the memory when she smelled something burning. *Oh crap, I forgot about the food.* She stirred the meat and vegetables as best as she could. After a month, Mackenzie still had trouble cooking. She either burned the food or didn't cook it long enough.

Mackenzie could hear John hammering. She smiled at the thought of him hammering at something without his shirt on. She turned back to the stove and stirred the burnt meat one more time. She went over to another cabinet and pulled open a can of Manwich sloppy joe mix. She used the little handheld can opener to open it and poured the sauce into the skillet with the burnt meat, stirring it. She let it simmer and stirred the vegetables that were sticking to the pot. She still heard John hammering away at something. She shook her head. *He sure is beating whatever it is to death.*

She went to the window and saw John hammering a board to the barn. She watched as he picked up another one and hammered it in. He moved to the other side of the barn and Mackenzie heard him hammering again. She turned back to the stove and turned the burners off. She walked to another cabinet and pulled out two plates and a package of hamburger buns. She heard the door open and John entered the room. He could tell that she had the burners up too high and had burned the food. He shook his head.

"Supper smells good. Can't wait to see what's for dessert." He came up behind Mackenzie and wrapped his arms around her. He nuzzled her neck, and she squirmed.

"Stop that, John. I'm trying to get our plates ready." He laughed softly in her ear.

"We could skip dinner and go straight to dessert." He kissed her neck, and she squirmed even harder. When he didn't release her, she kicked his shin. He let go in surprise, and she moved closer to the stove.

She laughed. "Now are you going to let me get our plates ready or am I going to have to kick you again?" He smiled.

"You might have to kick me again." When she moved to

kick him, he moved away and said, "Alright, alright. I'll let you get the food ready. Besides, I need to clean up." He walked up the stairs to the bathroom.

"Don't use all the water in the jug. I'll need it later." She smiled as she heard his laughter.

After dinner, John went to work on the wiring in the living room. Mackenzie decided to wash up. She had just finished when she heard John cussing downstairs. She frowned. *Where in the world did he learn those words?* She walked down the stairs and saw John holding his hand.

"John, what happened? Are you hurt?" John turned.

"I'm alright, Kenzie. Just a little shock." Mackenzie rushed the rest of the way down the stairs.

"Just a little shock! You could have been electrocuted. What in the hell were you thinking!?"

"Look I'm fine." He paused for a while. "I think we should call a plumber and electrician." Mackenzie shook her head.

"I think that is a good idea. Luckily my phone has a charge. I'll call in the morning. In the meantime, I want you to sit down and let me see that." John sat down on the foldout chair and Mackenzie grabbed the first aid kit from the kitchen. She came back and pulled his hand toward her. She flipped it one way and then the other. She kissed it and smiled at him.

"At least you're not burned. Don't ever scare me like that again." John got up from the chair and pulled her close.

He whispered in her ear, "I promise not to scare you like that again." He kissed her hard and lifted her up. He started walking up the stairs with her in his arms. He walked into the bedroom and laid her on the air mattress. He started kissing his way down. She giggled.

He smiled and said, "I think we are ready for dessert don't you?" Mackenzie laughed again, and he kissed her once more.

CHAPTER 8

John looked out the kitchen window at the cattle in the pasture. He smiled and went to make a pot of coffee for Mackenzie. He heard her upstairs turning on the shower and getting ready for the day. He had left the bedroom at dawn to take care of the animals. They were still sleeping on the air mattress and had no other furniture. Mackenzie thought it was a good idea that they go shopping for furniture.

They now had running water and electricity. He thought they could have done without electricity but knew that Mackenzie was used to having it. He remembered growing up helping his grandfather around the ranch and not using electricity as much.

Once the coffee was made, he poured two cups of coffee and put sugar and milk in Mackenzie's cup.

Mackenzie came down the stairs, and he handed her the cup.

"Thanks, cowboy. You ready to go furniture shopping?" She laughed when he groaned. "Come on; we need a proper bed and something to sit on besides metal chairs."

"Why do we need a bed and chairs? I like the air mattress. Less chance of you crawling away from me whenever you want." She smiled, and he kissed her. He sat on the foldout chair and pulled her onto his lap. Mackenzie sipped her coffee. John finished his second cup of coffee when they heard someone knocking.

"Who is that, John?"

"I don't know." He went to the door and saw someone standing with their back to the door. He opened the door. "Can I help you?" The man turned around, and John groaned.

"Been a while, John. I guess you remember me."

"How could I forget you, asshole. You got me fired!" Casey Maxwell smiled, his blonde hair spiked and still wearing the gaudy belt buckle that John had hated him wearing back at Running Steer, and waved to Mackenzie, who had come up to see who was at the door.

"Hello, Miss Tucker. How are you?"

Mackenzie scowled and ran at Casey. John caught her just before she could rake her nails across his face. "How dare you show your face here? How did you find us?"

"Woah, I was told where you might be by Max. I had no clue that you and John were together. I wanted to apologize to John for what I did. I quit working for Max when we couldn't get any more guests. I thought I could tell John I was sorry and ask for his forgiveness."

Mackenzie went limp in John's arms. "Why? You caused John trouble. You got him fired. Why should he forgive you?"

"Miss Tucker, I was jealous of him. I mean, he was a favorite of the guests. The only time anyone ever said they liked me was when I would tell the kids something interesting about the trail we were on. I was also jealous of the fact that he was always hanging around you."

"Kenzie, let me talk to Casey alone."

"But John….?"

"Please love, I need to talk to him alone without you hurting him." Mackenzie huffed off and went upstairs. John turned to Casey and closed the door behind himself.

Mackenzie looked out the upstairs window and watched John while he was talking to Casey. She wished she could hear what was being said. She shook her head. *How can he talk to that bastard? He got John fired from his job at Running Steer.* She jumped when she heard John laughing with Casey in the house. She rushed downstairs and found John patting Casey on the back.

"There you are, Kenzie. Casey is going to be working here. He is on a trial basis, but if he does a good job without causing trouble, he can have a permanent job." Mackenzie walked past John and slammed the front door behind her.

John and Casey cringed when they heard her gun the truck and rush out of the driveway. "Well, that could have gone better. Is she okay? Maybe I should have never come."

"Nonsense Casey. She is still sore about you getting me fired. It will pass. Besides, we planned to go shopping for furniture. She'll be back once she has calmed down. Let me show you what you will be working on."

Several hours later, John and Casey hear the truck return. They listen as Mackenzie closed the door of the truck.

"Should I go so that I don't get hurt?" John shook his head just as Mackenzie entered the kitchen. She paused in the doorway and looked from Casey to John. She finally looked straight at Casey.

"I want to apologize for my behavior earlier. Shall we start over?" Casey nodded.

"Welcome, Casey. I hope you are a big help around here."

"Thank you, Miss Tucker. I look forward to working for you." Mackenzie smiled and held her hand out to shake his.

"Please call me Mackenzie."

"Will do," Casey smiled and got up from the chair. "I better get back to work. I will see you at supper."

After Casey had left, Mackenzie turned to John. He opened his arms, and she rushed into them. He kissed the top of her head. "That was nice of you to apologize to him, babe."

"I'm sorry I was such a bitch. I calmed down after looking at furniture. I picked out a big bed for us as well as some good armchairs. I even picked out a few throw rugs. I think you'll like them."

"I'm sure I will. I learned that Max was sued."

Mackenzie stepped out of John's arms. "Who sued him?"

"One of the returning guests had heard that I was fired and sued him. That is the reason Casey is here. He quit when he heard that Max was going to be sued. Max had given Casey this address to come and persuade me to return, but Casey knew he had to apologize to me before I would even agree. He was right. However, I have this ranch and won't be able to work for him again, not that I would want to."

Mackenzie hugged him. "Well, I am glad you decided not to go back. Though I am worried about Gary."

"Casey said that the day Gary kicked his ass, he left afterward. He doesn't know where Gary is, but the others that were there went to other dude ranches."

"At least Casey has a job with us. I will have to get used to him being here." She paused and kissed him. "I love you."

"I love you too, love. Come on I could use a shower and want you to join me." Mackenzie laughed and followed John to the bathroom.

CHAPTER 9

Casey had been at the ranch for two months. Mackenzie liked having Casey helping them at the ranch. He seemed to have changed since coming there. He no longer creeped her out. He took over the cooking from Mackenzie. It turned out he could cook, which surprised John and Mackenzie.

That morning, Mackenzie walked into the kitchen and noticed that Casey wasn't sitting at his usual spot. She watched as John entered the kitchen with the bucket of eggs.

"Where is Casey?"

"He wasn't feeling well this morning, so he is resting."

"Alright. I will help you out today. I hope he feels better." She went to the coffee pot and poured herself a cup. She added the cream and sugar and sat down at the table.

John placed a plate of pancakes in front of her. She

smiled at him and dug in. She moaned when she tasted cinnamon in the pancakes. John smiled and kissed her head.

"Enjoy those pancakes, love. We have a big day ahead of us. We need to make sure that we have nothing that will get wet outside. We are supposed to have a big storm coming through tonight." She nodded and continued eating. He smiled again and put the eggs up in the fridge. He then went back outside to check on the cattle. *I hope Kenzie is up to the tasks today. Usually, she stays inside and only comes outside once in a while to watch me and Casey work.* He sighed and checked the fence.

After eating and washing her plate, Mackenzie went outside and found John by the fenced in pasture. He turned as she approached. "Good, you're here. I'm worried about one of the cows. She looks like she might give birth soon." Mackenzie nodded and looked at the cow in question.

She does look like she will give birth any minute now. Suddenly, the cow started making a loud racket. John jumped the fence and rushed to the cow.

"Kenzie, I need you to get a bucket of warm water and a washcloth. Go now. I'll get her inside the barn." Mackenzie turned and ran to get the water and cloth. She smiled. She couldn't believe that there would be a baby calf soon.

She went to the barn after getting what John wanted. She put it beside John. "Thank you, love. I can take care of it from here." She nodded and decided to check on Casey.

Mackenzie went to Casey's room and knocked.

"Come in." Mackenzie entered and found Casey sitting up in bed with the pillows behind him, reading. When it turned out that Casey was going to stay with them, Mackenzie went and bought him a bed.

"How are you feeling, Casey?"

"Could be worse." Mackenzie could tell it hurt Casey to talk.

"Would you like some soup? I could also make you something hot to drink."

Casey smiled. "That sounds good. Thank you, Mackenzie."

Mackenzie left the room to fix Casey a bowl of soup and a cup of hot chocolate. She looked out the window and saw the clouds gathering. *Those clouds look ominous. This mightbe a huge storm.* She opened a can of soup and put it in a bowl to heat in the microwave; John had bought for Mackenzie to use. She placed the cup of water for Casey's hot chocolate in the microwave after the soup was done to heat. Once that was done, she poured it over the cocoa mix and stirred. She took both the soup and cup of hot chocolate to Casey.

"Thank you, Mackenzie."

"You're welcome, Casey. I hope you get to feeling better." He nodded and she went to check on John. She found him washing his hands at the water spigot. She smiled and went to him but stopped when she saw the look on his face.

"John, what happened? Is she okay?" John shook his head sadly.

"The calf was stillborn, and the mother died afterward." Mackenzie paled,and John pulled her into his arms. He held her as she cried. *I wish I didn't tell her.* He sighed and noticed that he had tears in his own eyes. He let go of Mackenzie and turned around to wipe his eyes. He turned back to her and hugged her again. "Let's go inside and have lunch."

She pulled away. "What about the cow and her calf?"

"I already buried them away from the other animals. We don't want any predators attacking the others." Mackenzie nodded and walked toward the house. John followed her inside and closed the door.

That evening, John looked out the window at the storm clouds. He was glad that the animals were put away. Mackenzie was in the living room on the love seat, reading. They managed to get Casey to come out of his room. He was sitting in the armchair by the fire. He was wrapped up in a quilt from his bed.

John moved to the love seat and sat next to Mackenzie. He pulled her onto his lap and kissed her neck. She sighed and snuggled close to him. Suddenly there was a flash of lightning and John heard a cracking sound from outside.

Mackenzie jumped, and he hugged her closer. He let her go and went to look out the window.

"Holy shit, the cows are escaping!" Mackenzie jumped up from the love seat and rushed to get her boots on. John hurried over to her. "Are you sure you want to help with getting the cows?"

"This is my home, and I see those cows as a part of the family, so yeah, I want to help. Besides Casey is sick and shouldn't be out in this storm." John nodded and went to get the horses ready.

Mackenzie rushed outside, and John handed the reigns of her horse, Basil, which John had bought off of a neighbor, to her. She jumped on and galloped off to gather the cows. John followed her his bay, Jackson that he had gotten from a horse auction. They followed the cattle tracks until they hit the creek. The water of the creek was up to the horses' knees but still passable.

"John, are you sure we can find the cattle?" Mackenzie yelled over the thunder.

"We'll find them don't worry." John galloped faster. He looked back to see if Mackenzie was following him and saw lightning strike near the house. Suddenly he saw smoke rising at the ranch.

"FIRE!" John rushed past Mackenzie and headed toward the house. She followed him and saw the fire coming from the barn.

Please let the horses be okay. Mackenzie dismounted and rushed to get a bucket of water while John got the other horses out. She saw Casey on the porch with a bucket of water.

"You need to get back inside. Let me and John handle it, Casey." Casey shook his head, and Mackenzie sighed. *Typical male. Never listens.* She grabbed the bucket from him, rushed back to the barn and threw the water. She went back to the porch and handed off the empty bucket to Casey, who had another bucket ready for her. They repeated the process and John helped once he got the horses out. They managed to put the fire out but were not able to save the barn.

John shook his head as the sky began to clear and the full moon revealed the burned out barn. *At least I got the animals out,but I'm worried about the cattle.* Casey was laying down in the living room on the couch. Mackenzie was trying to keep the horses calm. John turned to the corral where the cattle were. He inspected where they had broken through and frowned.

"Kenzie, could you come over here please." Mackenzie walked over to him, and he pointed at the gate. "The cows didn't break through the gate. It wasn't even locked."

"Of course, it was locked. I made sure of it."

"Kenzie, that gate is wide open, and when the lightning struck, the cattle saw an opening and took it. I hate to say it, but you didn't triple check to see if it was closed and locked."

"John I know I closed and locked it."

"Look here! You left that gate wide open, and now we have no cows to sell when the time comes."

"Maybe we shouldn't have got those cows to begin with."

"Those cattle would have helped us keep the ranch!"

"Why? So they can be slaughtered when we sell them? That's what they are going for. They will be slaughtered so that we can live in the middle of nowhere."

"Maybe you shouldn't have come with me. You could have stayed in the big city, but you chose to come out here!"

Mackenzie glared at John. "Maybe I should have stayed in Chicago. In fact, I think I will go back. At least my condo was surrounded by neighbors and didn't have stinky animals nearby."

"Perhaps you should." John stared at her waiting to see what she would say. She looked at him and turned on her heel. She walked to the house, went inside and came back out with a suitcase. She walked past John and got in her car.

"John, I'm going back to Chicago. I don't know if I will be back." With that, she drove away without so much a second look back. He stood there and watched her go.

Once he could no longer see the car, he turned around and found Casey standing on the porch. John walked past him into the house and was about to close the door when he heard Casey say, "You should go after her. She did help you take care of everything while I was laid up in bed sick. I think she was the best thing for you."

He turned back to Casey and glared. When Casey did not say anything else, John went inside to the bedroom. He looked around the room and glanced at the bed. He went over to it and picked up the hairpin in the shape of a lasso. He sat on the edge and held the pin. He turned it over in his hand and squeezed. He laid back on the bed and closed his eyes. *Why did I yell at her? Now I might never see her again.* He sighed and fell asleep with his wet clothes on.

CHAPTER 10

It had been three weeks since Mackenzie left the ranch. She went through the days in a sort of haze. Natalie had been surprised when Mackenzie called her and said that she was back in town. She asked her to come back and work for her. Natalie agreed only because she was worried about the strain in Mackenzie's voice. She even sold her apartment to live with Mackenzie.

Mackenzie would wake up every morning thinking about what she would do at the ranch and then remember that she had left it. She walked through the house going from the living room and the bedroom.

Sometimes she would look toward the door and wait for someone who would not come. Christina tried her best to get Mackenzie out of the house but to no avail. The only people who could get her to at least sit outside was Natalie and Macy.

One day, Macy found Mackenzie in the armchair by the window, crying. Macy gathered her in her arms and let Mackenzie cry on her shoulder. They stayed that way for a while. Macy patted Mackenzie on the back and pulled away.

"Mackenzie Ann Tucker, you have got to stop this nonsense. Maybe he has been busy and hasn't had time to come for you. So you need to hold your head up and be positive."

Mackenzie looked up at Macy in disbelief. "How can you know that? I left him. He must have found someone else by now."

"Don't you ever say that!? That man loves you! He could never replace you." Mackenzie was surprised to hear Macy yell at her. In all the time she had known her, Macy never yelled, not even once. Macy took a deep breath and looked at Mackenzie.

"Why don't you come over for dinner? It will just be the two of us and Miss Natalie if you want. She has been a big help to you, and I like to think of her as my friend as well as yours. So what do you say?" Mackenzie smiled and nodded. "Good. Why don't the two of you come by around seven?"

"Okay, we will. And thanks, Macy. You are a true friend." She got up and hugged Macy.

"You're welcome, Mackenzie." Mackenzie walked Macy

to her car and watched her drive away. She went back inside and called Natalie, who was at the store, to tell her about Macy's invitation.

Mackenzie and Natalie arrived at Macy's at seven. Macy greeted them and led them into the dining room. Mackenzie was surprised to find the room was devoid of Egyptian décor.

"Macy, what happened to the décor? It looks plain."

"Oh, I was bored with looking at all those old replicas. I now find that dolphins are much more calming." Macy smiled and handed them both a glass of ginger ale. "Besides, you should see the bedroom. It is decked out in Western décor. You know Mackenzie that hairpin of yours inspired me to decorate the bedroom from the boring gray that Calvin had insisted was calming to bright and sunny colors." Mackenzie smiled and took a drink. They all sat down, and the servant brought out the meal.

Mackenzie picked up just as the doorbell rang. Macy smiled. "I'll get it." She rushed off and Mackenzie resumed eating.

Macy came back and grinned wide. "Look who I found on my doorstep." She stepped aside and John entered the room followed by Casey.

"John, what are doing here?" Mackenzie got up and stood in front of John.

"I came for you Kenzie. I made a mistake. I shouldn't have yelled at you for something that was my fault."

"What do you mean?"

"I yelled at you even though I was the one who left the gate open. I forgot that I had checked on the cattle before dinner and left the gate open. Can you ever forgive me?"

Mackenzie smiled with tears in her eyes. "Oh, John, of course, I forgive you. I shouldn't have left. I was angry and...."

John kissed her to stop her explanation. He pulled away and smiled. "No need to explain. Besides, the cattle came back. We rebuilt the barn, but it cost us a lot."

Casey spoke up. "We missed you, Mackenzie. John here kept looking toward the door every time we heard a car pass by. He would walk around the ranch and forget what he was doing."

"She didn't need to know that!" John turned back to Mackenzie. "Will you come home with us, Kenzie?"

"Yes, I will come home." John picked her up and swung her around.

"You know. I think it would be better if we didn't sell the cattle to be slaughtered. I thought we could open up our owndude ranch and keep the cattle. While I was at Running Steer, I noticed a few things out of place. I think with what I saw we could run a dude ranch that is better than Running Steer ever was. What say you John, Casey?"

Casey laughed. "Sounds like a plan to me." John nodded in agreement.

Natalie spoke up. "You don't mind one more person joining you, do you? I've always wanted to live on a farm, and since a ranch is like one, it sounds like it would be better than living here."

Mackenzie smiled. "The more, the merrier," Natalie smiled.

Casey held out his hand to Natalie. "Hi, I'm Casey Maxwell."

"Natalie Mitchell," Casey smiled and led Natalie outside. Mackenzie turned back to Macy and hugged her.

"Thanks, Macy. I'll miss you. Oh, and tell the others I'm sorry."

"Will do, Mackenzie. Call me once you guys get going on the dude ranch and maybe I might come out there as a guest."

"Sounds wonderful, Macy. I'll let you know as soon as it happens." Mackenzie hugged Macy one more time and walked out of the house with John.

He stopped her from getting into her car. "I missed you. Next time we fight, make sure to smack the hell out of me." Mackenzie laughed, and John kissed her. She sighed, knowing that no matter what the future would bring, she wanted it to be with John. She hugged him.

"I need to go back to my place and make arrangements to

sell it. It might take me a few months to sell it. Can you wait that long?"

"I think I can manage. Besides, I have Casey to help me get the ranch ready to accept guests. I plan on making the dude ranch feel authentic." Mackenzie smiled and got in her car. She waved goodbye to John and drove with Natalie to the condo. She couldn't wait to go back to the ranch and make it work with John. She smiled and told Natalie what it was like living in New Mexico.

CHAPTER 11

John picked up the last board and hammered it up. He stepped back and smiled. *Finished. This has to be the best-looking storage shed ever.*

"John, it's almost time. Are you about done?" John looked toward the house and saw Mackenzie standing on the porch with her hand shielding her eyes. He still couldn't believe that in just a few short months, they were about to open the ranch to the public. He smiled.

"I'm done, Kenzie. I'll be right in." Mackenzie walked back in the house and went upstairs to get ready. John put the hammer into the tool belt around his waist and walked toward the house. He paused on the porch and looked around at the ranch. *I hope this all works out.* He smiled and entered the kitchen.

"Sorry, I wasn't there to help you finish the shed. Mackenzie had me make sure the roof wasn't leaking. I told her that the roof was sound, but she had me check anyway."

"That's alright Casey. She's just nervous. Macy is going to be one of the first guests, and she is worried that Macy won't like it."

Casey grinned. "I think it will be okay. Macy seemed excited about it over the phone when she called."

"You talked to her?"

"Yep. You know. She was all for it when we decided to start the dude ranch." John nodded and went upstairs to get ready for the first wave of guests. He found Mackenzie putting the lasso hairpin in her hair.

He wrapped his arms around her and kissed her neck. "John you need to take a shower. You smell." He laughed and let her go.

"I don't think I have enough time to take a shower. After all, the guests will be arriving any minute now." Mackenzie sighed and pointed to the bathroom.

"Shower, now." He shook his head and moved to the bathroom door.

He turned back around. "I'll shower, but there is no guarantee that I will be ready when the guests arrive." Mackenzie threw a pillow at him, and he dodged. It hit the door jamb and John laughed. She threw another pillow, but it hit the bathroom door as John closed it.

John finished dressing and went downstairs. He looked out the window and saw only his Chevy 2500, Mackenzie's red Porsche, Natalie's little Volkswagen Bug and Casey's Ford F150. He found Mackenzie pacing in the living room. Natalie was sitting on the couch with Casey. They were watching Mackenzie as she paced.

"Mackenzie, calm down. They will be here just give them time." Natalie sighed when Mackenzie ignored her.

"Kenzie, love, don't stress. It will be alright." John walked over to her and held her still.

"They should have been here by now. Macy said she was coming at noon, and it is noon now."

"It will be fine. She will come." Just then they hear a car pull up the driveway. "I'll go check it out." John went to the door and saw Macy climb out of a Ford Mustang. She removed her Dolce & Gabbana sunglasses, the sunlight shining off her strawberry-blonde hair.

"John it's good to see you again. Gosh, this place is huge. Where's Mackenzie at?" Macy jumped when the front door slammed against the outer wall.

"Macy!" Mackenzie rushed down the porch steps and almost tackled Macy. They had hugged for a long time before Macy broke the embrace. She held Mackenzie at arm's length and looked at her.

"You look great. This place has really given you such a glow."

"Thanks, Macy. You look good too." They hugged again, and Mackenzie led her inside. John was about to follow them when a Harley Davidson motorcycle pulled up. The man on the bike got off and walked over to John.

"Can I help you?" John watched as the man slowly pulled off the helmet and shook his head.

"Long time, no see, John. I hoped that you would contact me, but you never did."

"Gary?" Gary Tanner grinned and pulled John into a bear hug. His medium length brown hair was tied back with a leather piece. His green eyes glinted in his happiness.

"Why didn't you tell me you were started your own dude ranch? I would have jumped at the chance to work with you again."

"Sorry about that Gary." John stared at Gary, trying to figure out what was different about him.

"Yeah, I got my ears pierced. I thought since I quit working for Max, I could live how I want to. However, after I got that done, I realized that how I wanted to live was to keep working. I tried my hand at working at a factory, but they didn't like the fact that I like guys. I even tried to get a job as a farm hand, but they turned me down when they found out that I was gay."

"That's horrible, Gary." They both turned when they heard Mackenzie behind them.

"Nice to see you again, Mackenzie. How are you doing?"

"I'm doing great. You look different, did you grow your hair out?" Gary smiled and nodded.

"Yep sure did. What do you think? I think it looks great. Sometimes I drive my motorcycle without my helmet, just to feel the wind blow through it."

"I think it looks nice. I noticed that your ears are pierced as well." Gary nodded. Mackenzie smiled. "Why don't you come in? We just opened and already have a guest." Gary followed Mackenzie inside, leaving John standing by Gary's bike, speechless.

What in the hell was that about? Gary seemed happier. While working at Running Steer, Gary was usually by himself and only ever talked to me. No one else there knew he was gay, except Max and me. John remembered Max telling Gary to keep the fact that he was gay a secret from the other men. *Of course, Max was only okay with Gary being gay as long as he kept it a secret.* He shook his head and went inside to see if Mackenzie and Natalie needed any help.

By six, the other guests had arrived and had settled in. Natalie was in the kitchen cleaning up after the meal while Mackenzie was getting the living room ready for the meeting of the guests. John stood outside with Gary at the horse corral.

"I was thinking of buying some more horses. That way

we have plenty of them around forthe guests as well as any other staff, we might hire."

"John, I need to tell you something. The only reason I am here is that I have nowhere else to go. I was evicted from my apartment because I didn't have a job. I came here hoping for a job and a place to live."

John looked at Gary in surprise. "Of course, you can work here. Kenzie would love to have you here. She was worried about you when Casey got here and said he didn't know where you were."

"Are you sure it's okay? I don't want to impose."

"You won't be imposing. I am begging you to stay, and I believe Kenzie would love to have you as well."

Gary smiled. "Thank you, John. You're a good friend."

"Any time Gary. Come on; we have a meeting with all of the guests to introduce them to the staff, and since you are going to work here, you are a part of the staff." John patted Gary's shoulder and entered the house.

Gary looked toward the stables and grinned. He was glad John was so understanding. He turned and walked into the house, going to the living room to meet the guests.

Mackenzie smiled at him as he sat down and he smiled back.

CHAPTER 12

The ranch was a success. Every guest, who stayed at the Broken Trail Dude Ranch, had the same thing to say about it. They loved the friendly staff and the wonderful activities.

Mackenzie had her hands full with booking guests and making sure everything ran smoothly. John loved showing the guests how to rope and what it was like to live on a ranch. He made sure they got to experience the ranch as if they were in the old west.

Gary loved interacting with the little kids who came with their parents. He would tell them all about the animals on the ranch. The adults loved the way Casey would joke with everyone and how he treated the kids as young adults. The teenagers that would stay with their parents found that Casey was easy to talk to.

Every night, Mackenzie, John, Casey, Gary and Natalie would plan a special activity with the guests. Sometimes it was a campout and at other times, it was a little bonfire. The guests would leave feeling relaxed. Pretty soon, the ranch became well known throughout New Mexico and the other states.

Mackenzie enjoyed watching the little kids playing outside. She wished to have kids one day but wasn't sure how John would feel about it. He never talked about having kids, and she didn't bring it up.

One day, Mackenzie was outside helping one of the younger guests when a familiar face appeared.

"Hello, Mackenzie."

"Jason?" Jason Harper smiled at Mackenzie, his blue eyes glistening in the light. As usual, his black hair was styled in the latest style. His suit was tailored to fit him perfectly. She couldn't believe her ex-boyfriend was there. "What are you doing here?"

"I heard so much about this place, and that someone called Mackenzie Tucker worked here. I just had to see for myself. You look great. Is this just a summer hobby or what?"

Before Mackenzie could reply, John appeared. He held out his hand to Jason. "Hi, my mane is John Daniels, but everyone calls me John. I am co-owner of this ranch."

"Nice to meet you, John. I'm Jason Harper."

"Nice to meet you. Have you been shown to your room?"

Jason smiled. "Yes, I have. You have such a lovely place here. I have a feeling I'm going to like it here." John led Jason to the stables to have him pick out a horse to ride while there. Jason looked back at Mackenzie and smiled. Mackenzie blushed and rushed inside the house. She almost ran into Gary but continued to the living room.

What is Jason doing here? This isn'tsomething he would do. Mackenzie looked out the living room window and watched as Jason tried to get on one of the horses. She saw Casey trying hard not to laugh. She shook her head and went to find Natalie.

All through dinner, Mackenzie would keep giving Jason sideways glances. She still wasn't sure why Jason was there, but she hoped to find out. After dinner, John led the guests to the bonfire that Gary and Casey had started. Mackenzie followed behind carrying the graham crackers, marshmallows, and chocolate bars for the kids to make s'mores.

"Alright. Tonight we have a special treat for the kids. We have the stuff to make s'mores. The adults can make some too if they want." John held out the sticks the kids could use to make their treat. Natalie passed out a marshmallow to everyone who wanted to make a s'more. The kids eagerly went to the fire to stick their marshmallows in the fire. Casey and Gary stood by in case any of the kids needed help and to make sure none of the kids fell into the fire.

"Mackenzie, could I talk to you?" Mackenzie looked over at Jason.

"Sure Jason. What is it?" Jason led her away from the fire and the guests.

"I have a position opening up at my advertising firm and was wondering if you might be interested in applying for it." Mackenzie was speechless. "You don't have to apply right away."

"Jason, I have a job here. I am co-owner with John. We started this ranch with Casey and Natalie's help. I can't just up and leave."

Jason looked stunned but quickly recovered. "I'm not asking you to leave. As I said, you don't have to decide right now."

Mackenzie stood there for a minute. "Let me think about it, please."

"Take your time," Jason smiled and placed his hand on her shoulder. He left it there for a minute and then walked to the house.

John watched as the new guest led Mackenzie away from the fire. *He seems overly friendly with Kenzie. Do they know each other?* John saw Casey and Natalie watching Mackenzie and Jason as well. Natalie was frowning while Casey glared at Jason. John went back to watching Mackenzie and the new guest. He watched as the man put his hand on Mackenzie and left it there. John felt his temper flare but stayed where he was. He sighed when he saw Jason going back to the house.

Mackenzie came over and joined John at the fire. "Do you two know each other, Kenzie?"

"Oh, he is an old friend. He worked for another advertising firm. We ran into each other a few times."

John looked into the fire. "He seemed very friendly with you." He glanced down at Mackenzie and kissed the top of her head.

"Hey, John we could use some help here." He turned to Gary, who was trying to get marshmallow out of one of the boys' hair.

"Excuse me, love. I better help Gary." He kissed Mackenzie and walked over to Gary just as the boy's parents walked over to help.

Mackenzie sighed. *I should tell John about Jason's proposal.* Mackenzie watched as Gary distracted the kid while John worked on getting the sticky marshmallow out of his hair. She winced as John managed to get it out. The parents thanked John and Gary. Gary nodded and walked over to Mackenzie.

"Well, that went well. It turned out one of the other kids was chasing him while holding a marshmallow on a stick and tripped over a rock. The funny thing was it reminded me of that time one of the kids visiting Running Steer had fallen in my lap and got mashed potatoes on his face." Gary laughed. He noticed that Mackenzie didn't laugh at the joke like she did back at Running Steer. He hoped she was feeling alright.

"I'm sorry, Gary. I'm not feeling well. I think I'll go to bed." Mackenzie walked off toward the house. John walked over to Gary.

"Is Kenzie okay? She has seemed out of it since the new guest arrived. Before he got here, she was excited about giving the kids a chance to make s'mores."

"I sure hope she is, John. She didn't laugh when I talked about that kid who fell into my plate of mashed potatoes like she did before. Maybe she is just tired. She works harder than the rest of us. She has to make sure the schedules are all in order, she books guests and makes sure we have plenty of food to feed all those guests. Not to mention, she does work around the ranch."

"You're right. She hasn't had a day to herself. It has been a little strained between us as well." John stared into the fire. "We should have Natalie take over some of Mackenzie's duties for a while. She hasn't ridden Basil, since before we became so popular. She deserves a break. I'll bring the subject up to her in the morning before the guests wake up. Goodnight, Gary."

"Night, John. Me and Casey will stay up to make sure the guests go to bed and make sure the fire is out before we retire."

"Alright, Gary. See you in the morning." John walked up to the house.

He walked in and went upstairs to the bedroom. He saw Mackenzie laying down on the bed with her clothes still on. He undressed her without disturbing her and laid her under the covers. She smiled in her sleep as he undressed without the light on. He crawled into bed after locking the door and pulled her to him. She snuggled closer to him, and he fell asleep listening to her breathing.

The next morning, John woke up to find that Mackenzie was not next to him. He got out of bed and dressed. He went downstairs and looked in the living room and kitchen for her. When he couldn't find her, he went outside to look for her.

"Good morning John. Looking for Mackenzie?" John turned to Casey, who was scowling.

"Yeah. Do you know where she is?"

"She left this morning with the guy named Jason. She's teaching him to ride in the pasture." Casey pointed to where Mackenzie was showing Jason how to steer his horse. Jason couldn't get the horse to go where he wanted. John shook his head.

"Thanks, Casey." John walked over to the fenced in pasture. As he got closer, he could hear Jason.

"Mackenzie, what am I doing wrong? This dumb animal won't listen to me."

"Of course, the horse won't listen to you. You have to speak nicely to her." Mackenzie looked over and saw John standing there with a strange look on his face.

"Morning John. I was just showing Jason how to ride."

"I can see that, Kenzie. Can I speak to you privately for a moment?"

"Sure. Excuse me, Jason. I'll just be a minute." Mackenzie rode over to the fence, tied the reins of Basil to a pole and hopped off. She climbed the fence and almost fell. John caught her and held on for a while. He kissed her on the lips in front of Jason, keeping her close to him. When they broke apart, John led Mackenzie away from Jason's hearing.

"Kenzie, I think you should let Natalie take over your duties for a few days. You deserve to relax and not worry about anything."

"I can't John. There are too many things that need to get done." Mackenzie tried to walk away, but John grabbed her arm.

"Please, Kenzie. Everyone is worried that you are over-working yourself. I know you want to be useful, but you're just hurting yourself by taking on so many responsibilities. All I'm asking is for you to take a few days off and let Natalie take over. If it gets to be too much for her,

I'm sure Casey will be willing to help her. Besides, Casey knows a lot about running a dude ranch. Before I started working at Running Steer, Casey would help Max with running the place. So, will you take a few days off?"

Mackenzie nodded, knowing she deserved a break from all the things she would do to keep the place running smoothly. "I'll take a few days off on one condition."

"Anything you want, love just as long as you relax."

"I want to participate in the activities the guests do."

"Of course. I did say anything you wanted." John kissed her and held her for a bit. He let her go and walked back to the house. *At least she is taking a break. I need to find Natalie and let her know.*

Mackenzie watched as John walked back to the house. *That was sweet of him to worry about me. I hope Natalie can handle everything.* She felt Jason's hand on her shoulder.

"Is everything okay?"

She turned toward him. "Yeah. He was just telling me that I need to take a few days off. I overwork myself and never have time for a break, so he is letting someone else do my duties for the next few days."

"Well, that's good. Why don't you hang out with me? It'll be fun."

"Sure. Come on. Breakfast is about to start, and I need to see Natalie make sure she is up to taking over my duties." Mackenzie walked back to the fence to retrieve Basil.

During breakfast, Mackenzie sat with the guests. Jason

sat beside her. They talked about what they had been up to since they last saw each other. John sat next to Gary, who was frowning. John clenched his fists every time Mackenzie laughed at Jason's jokes.

"Are you okay, John? You look like you're about to punch the guy." John turned to Gary.

"I'm fine. What could she see in him? This morning he called his horse a dumb animal. That pissed me off."

"I've seen this thing before. Casey used to look at you the way you are looking at that guy back at Running Steer. You're jealous of the guy."

"I am not jealous."

Gary grinned. "You are so jealous. The green-eyed monster has a hold of you. Don't worry. He'll leave, and you will have Mackenzie back. Don't forget that she loves you. It will work out, trust me."

"I hope you're right." John continued watching Mackenzie and Jason. Mackenzie looked over and smiled at John. *I really hope Gary is right. I would hate to punch the guy. I mean, we could lose the ranch if I hurt one of the guests on purpose.*

Mackenzie spent the day hanging out with Jason and the other guests. She enjoyed the activities along with the guests. After lunch, John taught all the guests how to use a lasso. Mackenzie joined in and helped some of them when they asked. John used Mackenzie as a demonstration to show

how to swing the rope. The guests clapped when Mackenzie got the rope around the horns of the hay bale. Jason clapped the loudest. John gritted his teeth and nodded to Mackenzie. She was stunned at his behavior. *I know Jason is a bit melodramatic, but that is no excuse for John to be angry.* Mackenzie sighed and went back to stand by Jason. She didn't indicate that she heard Jason congratulate her.

The rest of the day passed without any incident with the guests. However, Mackenzie checked on Natalie a few times. Natalie would shoo her away and tell her to have fun. Mackenzie would laugh and leave but would come back a few minutes later. Casey finally had to come and help Natalie get rid of Mackenzie. They locked her out of the office and took her keys away. She went back to the activities but tried to convince Gary to check on Natalie for her and report back. Gary refused.

"Mackenzie, today is your day off. You need to relax. There is no point in worrying. Besides, I'm helping as well." Mackenzie nodded. Gary pushed her, and she bumped into John.

"Here you go, boss. She's all yours." Gary laughed and walked off. John grinned and led Mackenzie over to the stables.

"I know I'm supposed to be working, but I thought you might want to go riding with me. Gary is taking over for a bit so that we could have time to ourselves."

"Oh, John. I wish I could but remember I'm a guest today." She smiled and kissed him. He laughed and swung her around. They broke apart when someone cleared their throat.

"Hey, Mackenzie. The next activity is about to begin. We need to head over and join in." Jason stood there with a sour look on his face.

"Oh yeah, forgot about that. Sorry, John. I've got to go." Mackenzie left with Jason. John stood there and watched them walk off. He shook his head in anger and stomped off. Gary turned the corner of the stable and almost bumped into John.

"What happened? I thought you two were going riding?" John pushed past Gary, almost making him fall.

"I changed my mind." John stomped off toward the house and slammed the front door.

Natalie jumped when she heard the door. She left the office and saw John head upstairs. "I thought you and Mackenzie were going riding?" John ignored Natalie and slammed the bedroom door. Natalie shook her head and went back to do the paperwork.

At dinner, John was quiet and glared at Mackenzie and Jason. She could feel his anger and tried to avoid looking at him, but her eyes kept moving to look at him. When she saw the look on his face, she excused herself and walked over to John with her plate. Gary gave up his seat to

Mackenzie, and she sat down. John continued staring away from her. She sighed and resumed eating. Soon John grabbed her free hand and held it. He rubbed his thumb against the back of her hand. She sighed and looked at him. He smiled, and she relaxed.

He leaned down and whispered in her ear. "I'm sorry I was so rude. Can you ever forgive me?" She squeezed his hand in response. He smiled again, and she smiled back. They sat like that until they were the last ones at their table.

Mackenzie was the first one to break the silence. "I'm sorry too. I know I am hanging out with Jason. I should have declined when he came to get me for the next activity. I'm sorry."

"That is understandable. You did, after all, want to be treated like a guest."

"I don't think I am cut out to be a guest again. It just feels weird."

John smiled. "I have an idea. How about we have our own little campout. We can go to the pond and camp under the stars there. Just you and me. What do you say?"

"I would love to John. Just let me grab a few things and I will meet you at the stables."

He kissed her. "I'll be waiting." He got up and walked outside. She went upstairs, grabbed the big sleeping bag and packed a bag with a few things they might need and went to the stables. She passed Gary on the way to the stables, and he winked at her. She grinned and continued to the stables. She found John with Basil and his horse, Jackson saddled and ready to go. They got on their horses and rode to the pond. Once there, John set up the sleeping bag while Mackenzie gathered some sticks for a fire. They could hear the kids and adults laughing at something Casey or Gary did. *The full moon is so beautiful out here. I'm glad John wanted to do this. It will be nice to sleep outside under the stars and the moon.*

John started the fire and pulled Mackenzie close. He kissed her until they were both breathless. They sat staring at the fire until they could hear the guests getting ready to go to bed. John smiled, knowing that Gary would make sure no one would stay up and wind up stumbling upon him and Mackenzie.

Once it got quiet and all they could hear was the crickets, they got undressed and crawled into the sleeping bag. They made love under the stars and fell asleep in each other's arms.

CHAPTER 13

The next morning, John, Mackenzie, and Gary saw the guests off. Jason walked over to Mackenzie and waited for her to finish with one of the guests.

"Well, I need to be off. I have to get back to work. Have you thought about the job offer?"

"I was so busy I forgot about it. I'm sorry. I need to think about it." *I completely forgot about his job offer.*

"Like I said, take your time. When you've thought about it, call me. The number is still the same."

"I will. I'll see you." She gave Jason a quick hug and waved goodbye as he drove away. John came up behind her and wrapped his arms around her.

"What was that all about, love?"

"He just wanted to tell me that he liked it here and might

be back next year." John looked down at her and kissed the top of her head. *I can't believe I lied to him. I want to tell him about the job offer,but I'm not sure how he will react.* John released Mackenzie and went to check on the horses.

Mackenzie sighed and went inside to make sure the rooms were clean and ready for the next wave of guests.

Natalie was in the office working on the schedule when she heard a car pull up. "I think we have our first guests!" Mackenzie came out of one of the rooms and looked out the living room window.

"I think you're right, Natalie. I hope John is still outside with the horses." Mackenzie and Natalie walked outside just as John came out of the stables. Behind the car was a few more cars. "Yep looks like our guests have arrived." The cars stopped, and people started to get out.

"Welcome to the Broken Trail Dude Ranch. We are glad you are here. Tonight before dinner, we will have a meet and greet. It will help us get to know you and vice versa. Until then, feel free to explore. If you have kids, make sure they know to be careful around the animals. Thank you for choosing our ranch for your vacation." John walked around and shook everyone's hands, even the little kids. Mackenzie smiled and talked with the guests to arrange their rooms. Gary and Casey talked to the kids, making them laugh. Natalie passed out the schedules to the adults and pointed out special activities for kids to the parents.

After John had shaken everyone's hands, he walked over to Mackenzie and whispered in her ear. "Before the meet and greet, meet me at the back of the stables for a special treat," Mackenzie smiled and kissed him.

"EWWWWWW!" They both laughed at the kids who yelled. The parents laughed as well. John smiled and walked toward the back of the stables. Mackenzie smiled and showed the guests their rooms so that they could unpack if they wanted.

Once she was done helping the guests, Mackenzie walked to the back of the stables. There she found John holding open one of the storage rooms to the stables.

"Right this way, ma'am." Mackenzie giggled and walked into the room. She gasped. The room was lit with candles, and there was a blanket on the floor with a bowl of strawberries and a bottle of wine chilling in a bucket of ice. *What is all this?*

"Happy birthday, love." John wrapped his arms around her and kissed her neck. *I can't believe he remembered. When did he set this up and why didn't I notice?* Suddenly she remembered that he had goneto the stables after the last guests left by himself. She also remembered that Casey didn't see the guests off that morning. *Of course, he enlisted Casey's help with this. Very sneaky.*

"Thank you, John. The funny thing is I forgot that it was my birthday." John smiled and sat down on the blanket with her on his lap. He opened the bottle of red wine and poured it into two glasses. He handed her one and set his down.

"Gary and Casey are keeping the guests busy and away from here so that we can have some time to ourselves. I thought we could celebrate without Natalie and them. I wanted this to be special."

"Oh, John it's absolutely perfect. How did you know I love strawberries?"

"You told me four months ago when we found that farmer's market in the nearby town. You said that you loved them because they were your favorite color. I had sent Casey to the store early this morning to buy them."

"I'm glad you did. You and Casey gave no indication of what you were doing." John smiled and took a sip of his wine. He picked up a strawberry and fed it to her. She moaned when she bit into it. He smiled and kissed her. He kissed her eyes, her nose, and her mouth. They fell back on the blanket. He made her feel loved as he made love to her. They laid on the blanket, feeling content and fell asleep.

After cleaning up the room, John and Mackenzie went into the house for the meet and greet. They entered the living room just as Natalie came into the room with some snacks for the kids.

"So did you two have fun?" Natalie laughed at the mortified look on Mackenzie's face. "That answers my question. We are almost ready for the meeting. Why don't you two get ready? We don't want the kids asking questions about why you two look sloppy." John and Mackenzie looked at each other and laughed.

John then nodded to Natalie and went upstairs with Mackenzie to get ready. They came back downstairs looking more presentable as the guests entered the living room.

Once all the guests arrived, Gary and Casey entered.

Gary winked at Mackenzie while Casey grinned at her. She blushed. John reached over and hugged her. He stood up and addressed the guests.

"Again, thank you all for coming. I'm John Daniels, but you may call me John. This ranch was my grandfather's but is now mine. I decided to turn it into a dude ranch with three of the people you see here. I'll let them introduce themselves."

Mackenzie stood up. "Hi my name is Mackenzie Tucker, but everyone calls me Mackenzie. I would like all of you to call me Mackenzie but that is up to you. I help run the day to day activities and will participate in them when I get free time. I hope you enjoy it here and if you have any questions feel free to ask." She sat down and Natalie got up to introduce herself. Next, Casey got up and introduced himself. Last, Gary introduced himself and told them that if the kids wanted, they could ask him to hang out with them during the bonfires and campouts.

"Now it is your turn to introduce yourselves." One by

one, the guests introduced themselves. Once they were done, Natalie led them outside to the bonfire area where a bonfire was already started.

The guests were served and sat around the bonfire eating. The kids all sat next to Gary. He smiled and told jokes. A few of the adults sat next to Mackenzie and John. One of the women near them, who had introduced herself as Kelsey Grayson asked, "So how long have you been running this ranch?"

"We have only been running it for a few months. Before we were using it as a regular ranch until we decided it would be easier to turn it into a dude ranch. In fact, me, Gary and Casey worked at another dude ranch in Nevada, and we met Mackenzie when she was there to help the ranch get advertising on the radio."

"How did you get from working on a different dude ranch to opening this one?"

Why is she asking all these pointed questions? Why would she care how we got started? John looked at Mackenzie. She shook her head, and he shrugged. "It's complicated. Suffice it to say; there were problems at the other ranch, and we moved out here." That answer seemed to satisfy the woman, and she didn't ask any more questions.

After dinner, Mackenzie and John excused themselves and went to find Gary. They found him laughing with a few of the kids.

"Excuse us kids but we need to talk to Gary, please. We'll give him back once we get done talking to him." The kids nodded and Gary got up to walk with John and Mackenzie.

"What is it, guys?"

"We are going to bed and wanted to make sure that you can get all the guests to bed before midnight and remind them about what time to wake up."

"Sure, John, Mackenzie. By the way, Mackenzie.

Happy birthday. Now go, sleep and goodnight."

Mackenzie smiled and hugged Gary. "Goodnight, Gary. See you in the morning. And thank you." Gary smiled, and John patted his shoulder. They walked to the house and went upstairs. They got undressed and fell asleep.

The next morning, John let Mackenzie sleep in. He went downstairs quietly and found Gary and Casey whispering in the kitchen.

"Is something wrong guys?" John asked in a whisper. Gary looked at John and pointed out the window. John looked out and saw the woman named Kelsey on one of the horses. "What is she doing?"

"We came from our rooms and saw her out there. We've been watching her, and she hasn't done anything wrong. Perhaps you should go out there and ask what she is doing?" John nodded and went outside. The woman stopped what she was doing and waited for John to reach her.

"Excuse me but what are you doing? We usually have the

guests sleep until seven and then have them down for breakfast."

"Oh I know, I read the schedule. I'm used to getting up early. My parents used to own a dairy farm, and I helped them in the morning before going to school. We also kept horses, so I know my way around a horse."

"What made you decide to come here?"

"Well, it has been a while since I have ridden a horse. I work at a law firm and haven't been on a farm since becoming a lawyer. I thought that if I went to a ranch, I could get back to my roots for at least a little while." John nodded. *I remember the feeling. I felt that way after I was fired from the rodeo.*

"Well, I will leave you to it. Just make sure at least I or one of the guys knows that you are up."

"Will do. Sorry for causing you trouble."

"It's no trouble at all and welcome to Broken Trail." John waved and went to check on the cattle.

Every morning, John would find Kelsey riding in the horse corral early. Some mornings, John would join her in the corral and sometimes they would go riding close to the main buildings. Sometimes Mackenzie would find John just talking to her while she rode. Every time she saw them together, it felt like John was betraying her. She hated that feeling. She had asked Natalie if she ever felt that way about someone. Natalie just looked at her and shrugged.

One day, John was at the cattle pen about to brand the cattle. Earlier he tried to get Mackenzie to help, but she refused. She told him that he shouldn't brand them because she knew it must hurt the cows to be burned. He told her it needed to be done, but she didn't listen.

Mackenzie finally left John to the task. He was having trouble with the last cow when Kelsey came up.

"Need help?"

"Sure could, thanks." Kelsey hopped over the fence and held her hand out for the brand. He handed it to her, and she talked calmly to the cow. While the cow was distracted by her voice, she stuck the brand to its flank. It didn't make a sound when the hot brand touched it.

"How did you do that!?" She smiled and put the brand back in the coals.

"When I was in high school, my parents sold our dairy cows and bought some steers. They were having trouble branding them, so I went over to help. I was just talking to the steers when my dad stuck them while I was talking to them. It turns out I have a way with keeping animals calm with my voice."

"Well, that was a big help." John patted her on her shoulder. They walked back to the house, laughing about how one day when Kelsey was in high school, she had punched a guy for picking on another student and had broken his nose.

Mackenzie watched as John touched Kelsey. They

started walking back to the house,and she saw John laughing at something Kelsey said. *How dare she come here and try to take John from me. She has been too friendly with him.* Mackenzie turned away from the living room window and locked herself in the office. She refused to come out for lunch and dinner, saying she had too much paperwork to do. When everyone went outside to the bonfire, Mackenzie went upstairs and fell asleep. John came in the bedroom after a while and got undressed. He climbed into the bed and tried to cuddle with Mackenzie. She stiffened, scooting further away on the bed. John sighed, turned over and fell asleep as well.

CHAPTER 14

John woke up the next morning to find that Mackenzie wasn't in bed. He got up and dressed. He went downstairs and looked in the office. The only person in the office was Natalie.

"You're up earlier than usual, Natalie. Have you seen Kenzie this morning?" Natalie looked up from the papers she was working on.

"I decided to help Mackenzie with the paperwork this morning. I haven't seen her, though. Maybe Casey or Gary saw her."

"Thanks, Natalie." John left the office and found Gary at the staff table, drinking a cup of tea. "Morning Gary. Have you seen Kenzie?"

"She went to the stables a while back. Why?"

"She wasn't in bed when I woke up. I'm worried about her. She was angry about something yesterday."

"Well, she seemed fine to me this morning. She smiled and hugged me. She told me that she was going for a ride and then be back in time for breakfast. Perhaps you could catch her before she gets too far."

"Thanks, Gary." John went outside to the stables. He looked in Basil's stall and found it empty. He went to Jackson's stall and saddled him. As he was leading his horse out, Mackenzie came riding up on Basil. She stopped as soon as she saw John. She sat there for a minute and then dismounted. She walked past John into the stables. He followed her and watched as she unsaddled Basil and gave her a rub down.

Once she was done, Mackenzie walked to John and kissed his cheek. "Good morning, honey. I hope I didn't worry you. I'll see you at breakfast. I want to take a shower before I eat. I had a long ride to clear my head."

"Are you okay, Kenzie? You seemed mad about something last night."

Mackenzie laughed. "I was still angry this morning which is why I went for a ride. I figured out that I was angry for no reason." She kissed him again and went in the house.

He stood there for a while and then shook his head.

She seems okay. Maybe I was worried for nothing. He

put Jackson back in his stall and went inside to start the coffee for the guests.

Mackenzie talked all through breakfast about her ride. She was smiling and joking with Gary and Casey. She would glance at John now and then and smile. She noticed that the woman that John had been hanging out with was not at breakfast.

After helping Natalie wash the dishes, Mackenzie went outside to get some fresh air. She waved to the guests who said good morning to her. She smiled. *It is days like this that I am glad we started this business. The guests enjoy being here and that makes me happy.* She sighed in contentment. She watched as John taught the little kids how to rope. She smiled when he looked her way. He would smile back and turn back to the kids.

Mackenzie frowned. *I wish I knew if John wants kids. He is so good with them, but he has never said if he wants to have them.* She sighed and went back inside.

She sat in the office before lunch and was working on some more paperwork. Suddenly there was a knock on the office door.

"I'll be with you in a moment."

"Take your time. I can wait." Mackenzie started. She looked up and saw Jason standing in the doorway. He smiled at her and leaned against the doorjamb, his dark blue designer suit pressed to perfection as usual.

"Jason, what are you doing here?"

"I was just passing through and thought I would see if you thought about the job offer."

"Jason..." Mackenzie stared at John who was standing behind Jason.

"Kenzie, what job offer is he talking about?"

Jason turned toward John. "I offered her a job at my advertising firm. If I don't fill it soon, it will be filled before I can. Did she not tell you?" Jason walked past John who followed him with Mackenzie behind him. John glared at Jason.

He turned to Mackenzie. "Why didn't you tell me?"

"John, I..." Just then Kelsey came down the stairs.

"I'm sorry I missed breakfast. I slept in without meaning to." She looked from Mackenzie to John and then to Jason. "Did I miss something?"

Mackenzie's face turned red in anger. "I was going to tell you, but you were hanging around your little mistress there. I even wanted to tell you before she showed up and started flirting with you."

"What about you? You were hanging all over that guy while he was here last time. Don't think I didn't notice him hitting on you and you letting it happen. So excuse me if I am nice to a guest. At least, I could talk to her about working with cattle. You wouldn't even help me brand our cattle. She at least got in the pen with me and helped brand the last cow

I was having trouble branding BY MYSELF no thanks to you. So go. Take the job offer. When it fails, don't come crying to me." With that, John stomped outside. Luckily, Gary and Casey had taken all the guests on a ride on the north side of the ranch. He went to the stables, saddled Jackson and exited the stables on Jackson's back. Mackenzie ran out of the house with tears in her eyes.

"Where are you going?"

"I'm going to check on the fence on the south side of the ranch. I don't know when I'll be back. If I get back before dinner, you better not be here." He kicked Jackson's sides and went galloping off.

"JOHN!!!" Mackenzie stood there with the tears running down her face.

"Well, that should have gone better." Jason took Mackenzie by her shoulders and turned her to him. "So will you take the job?"

Mackenzie pushed him away. "I'm sorry Jason, but I won't be taking the job. I need to be here to run the place while John is gone."

"Are you sure? You would get your own office with a view and health insurance. You couldn't ask for more. Besides, I still love you and would love to have you work for me with even more benefits." He grabbed Mackenzie and kissed her hard. She pushed him away and punched him in the nose.

His nose started bleeding. He stared at her in surprise. "You broke my nose!"

"Serves you right, asshole. I may have loved you once, but now I love John. Now thanks to you I might, never see him again. So you can take your job and stick it up your ass!" Mackenzie stomped off into the house. She stopped when she saw Natalie staring at her and smiling.

"What!?"

Natalie burst out laughing, and Mackenzie started laughing with her. Once they caught their breath, Mackenzie started crying again. Natalie hugged her and patted her back. "It will be alright. He is just angry and needs to let off some steam. He'll come back."

Once Mackenzie's sobs quieted down, Natalie led her into the kitchen. She made Mackenzie sit at the small kitchen table and went to the cabinet to get the hot cocoa mix. She put some water in the kettle and placed it on the stove. She poured the mix into a mug and once the water was ready, she poured it in as well. She stirred it and handed it to Mackenzie.

Mackenzie held the mug without taking a drink; Natalie sat beside her. They sat there until Mackenzie took a sip. She sighed and drained the cup. She smiled at Natalie and got up from the table. "I'm going to lay down. Please make sure no one disturbs me. I might not come down for lunch or supper. If I don't, could you bring me something?"

"Of course. If John comes back, do you want me to send him up?"

"No. Just tell me when he gets back, and I'll come down." Natalie nodded, and Mackenzie went upstairs and laid down.

At lunch, Natalie came up and put the plate of food on the bedside table. Mackenzie didn't stir, and Natalie left quietly. Again at dinner, Natalie came upstairs and noticed that the lunch plate only had one bite taken out of everything on the plate. She took that plate and put the dinner plate in its place. She shook her head and left Mackenzie alone.

CHAPTER 15

Mackenzie slept for a little bit more and woke up around midnight. *John should have been back by now. I hope he still isn't mad at me.* She picked up the plate Natalie had left and gone downstairs. She put it in the kitchen and was about to leave when Kelsey came in. Mackenzie glared at her.

"Please, I want to talk. I need you to know a few things. Please." Mackenzie scowled but gestured to the table. They both sat down, and Kelsey sighed. "I know you probably hate me, but you need to know that I do not have that kind of feelings for John. In fact, I think of him as an older brother that I never had."

Mackenzie couldn't believe what she said. "Really?"

"Of course. I could never have those kinds of feelings for

him. I mean, I already have a fiancé. I wanted to come out here by myself before I got married to enjoy being around horses and cattle again. Me and my fiancé work at rival law firms and plan to open our own law firm once we are married."

"I hope it all works out for you and your fiancé. I'm sorry for accusing you of trying to take John from me. I was so jealous of the way he could talk to you about everything to do with running a ranch. It felt has if my heart would break. To tell you the truth, I had already planned on turning that job offer down. I love it too much here. I love hanging out with the guests especially the kids. I want to have kids of my ownsomeday, but I'm not sure if John would want to. I guess I want him to be the one to ask to have kids."

"I can understand that. I wanted to have kids too but wasn't sure if my fiancé wanted to have some. Finally, I asked him and it turned out that he wanted to have kids, but he was afraid that I wouldn't." They both laughed.

After a while, Mackenzie got to know more about Kelsey. It turned out that she liked the color red too. Mackenzie learned that Kelsey used to race horses as well as help her parents on their farm. Mackenzie told her about the first time she had met John, Casey, and Gary. They laughed when Mackenzie told her about the kid who had gotten the marshmallow in his hair. It was almost dawn when they got done talking.

Kelsey got up and stretched. "Well, I'm leaving this morning. I need to get packed."

Mackenzie got up. "I need to find John and tell him that I didn't take the job and apologize to him."

"Would you like me to come with you halfway?"

"Thanks, that would be nice. Do you know where he might have gone?"

Kelsey thought about it. "He told me how far away the southern fence is when we were riding together. I can point you in the right direction."

"That would be fine. Let's go." They both went outside and got the horses saddled. They started riding in the direction John had taken when he had left. They rode for about two hours when Kelsey stopped.

"I need to head back. I think if you keep along this path, you will run into the fence. If he isn't at the part of the fence you run into, ride parallel to the fence until you find him. When I get up to the house, do you want me to tell Gary or the other two where you are?" Mackenzie shook her head, and Kelsey turned around. She waved to Mackenzie and rode off. Mackenzie kept riding in the direction Kelsey pointed.

Several hours later, Mackenzie stopped to rest. *I should have brought something to drink. I'm not sure I will find him. He might never want to see me again.* Mackenzie sighed andwas about to ride some more when she heard a rattling sound. Basil screamed and took off. Mackenzie held on and tried to stop her horse.

"Basil, slow down. Whoa!" Basil ignored her commands and kept running when Mackenzie's grip on the reigns slipped. Basil stopped suddenly, and Mackenzie was thrown over her head. Basil ran off in the direction they had come from.

"Basil come back." Mackenzie got up and ran after Basil. She tried to keep up but kept losing sight of her horse. Finally, she stopped and rested. She looked around her and didn't recognize her surroundings. She walked for a bit, but the sun was too hot.

I can't believe Basil threw me. She has never done that before. Now, I have no clue where I am. She sighed and continued walking. Suddenly, she stepped in a hole and fell. She caught herself before she could fall on her face. *Damn hole. Why did I have to trip?* She got her foot out of the hole and tried to walk on it. She fellin pain. She started crying. Every time she tried to move, the pain would shoot up her leg. *Where is John? I wish I had never said what I did. I should have told him about Jason's job offer. I just wish John would findme.* She sighed and closed her eyes. She fell asleep with her left leg stretched out to keep it from hurting.

It was dark by the time Mackenzie woke up. She shivered and moved her left leg. She winced as the pain shot from her ankle and up her leg. *How long have I been out here?* Suddenly she heard the coyotes' howling. She tried to crawl away from the direction they were howling but stopped in pain. *I'll never be able to get away from the coyotes. I should have had Kelsey tell Gary and them that I was out here.* Mackenzie started crying again and screamed when she felt something grab her arm.

"Kenzie, Kenzie, it's me. It's John." John pulled her close to his chest. He felt her wince when he moved her. "Are you alright? What happened?" Mackenzie clung to John and sobbed into his shirt. He held her and let her cry. "It's alright. I'm here, baby. You're safe."

When her crying stopped, she looked up at John but could barely see him. "John, is it really you? I'm not dreaming am I?"

"No babe, it's not a dream. I'm right here and I'm not leaving you,but I need to get a few things from Jackson's saddle. I'll be right back." John released her and walked over to his horse. He grabbed the flashlight, a blanket, a bedroll and his water. *I'm gladI already had my saddle ready. I had already planned on checking the fence yesterday before that whole fiasco. When I heard the howling, I knew something was in trouble. I never thought it would be Kenzie.*

"John, where are you? Please don't leave me!" He hurried over to her and held her.

"I'm right here. I said I wouldn't leave you." He spread out the bedroll and blanket on the ground. "Now, I'm going to move you onto the bedroll. I will try not to bump your leg but I need you under the blanket." He picked her up as gently as he could and placed her under the blanket. She winced and cried out when he moved her leg under the blanket.

"I'm sorry babe. You're freezing, and I need to get you warmed up. I'm going to turn on the flashlight so that you can see that I haven't left you." He turned on the light and handed it to her. "There you go. Why did you come all the way out here?"

"I had to find you and apologize for my behavior yesterday. I should have told you about his job offer, but I never got around to it. We were so busy that I forgot. I turned down his offer, and when he kissed me, I punched him and broke his nose." She had the flashlight facing away from his

face but could see his face. She watched as he tried hard not to laugh. He was finally able to keep a straight face after a few attempts.

"Well, I think I should apologize too. I should not have yelled at you. I should have asked you about what he had wanted the first night he was there. I could tell you were upset but never thought to ask. Can you forgive me, again?"

Mackenzie nodded and then hit his arm. "What was that for?"

"After we had our first fight, you told me to hit you next time we fought." He laughed and kissed her. He tried to pull away, but she wrapped her arms around his neck. "Please, promise me that you won't ever leave me." He nodded and kissed her. He ran his hands through her hair. She sighed as his tongue touched hers. He pulled her even closer. They broke apart after a while, breathless. She snuggled close to him as best as she could with her leg. She laid her head on his chest and listened to his heartbeat.

"John?"

"Yes, baby."

"I was wondering how you felt about having kids."

John thought about it for a bit. "Well, to tell you the truth, I haven't really thought about it. But I do know that if you want to have kids, I would want to be the one to give them to you." He waited to see what she would say but noticed that she was asleep. He smiled, laid his head on hers and fell asleep as well.

The next morning, John woke up to people shouting.

"Found her. John's with her." John opened his eyes and saw Gary rushing to them, his face haggard. John moved slightly, and Mackenzie opened her eyes.

"What's going on? Did something happen?"

"It's alright. Gary and the others are here. You're safe."

He sat up and yelled, "Kenzie's hurt. I think she broke her ankle!" Gary rushed over with a first aid kit. He touched her leg, and she winced.

"She didn't break her ankle. She sprained it. Once we wrap it up, she will have to use crutches or be carried everywhere. She'll be fine." Gary got the gauze out and wrapped her ankle as gently as he could.

"Are we going home, John? Please tell me we are going home."

John looked down and smiled. "Yes we are, and the first thing we are going to do is put you in a warm bath." He kissed the top of her head just as Gary finished wrapping her ankle. John picked her up and carried her over to Jackson. He placed her in the saddle, then got up behind her.

"Hold on. This might hurt." He flicked Jackson's reins and rode to the house at a walk. Gary picked up the bedroll, blanket, and dead flashlight and put them on his saddle. He followed them to the house with the guests who had volunteered to find Mackenzie.

When they made it back to the house, Natalie rushed out with Casey to meet them, both of them looking like they didn't sleep. Casey helped Mackenzie off the saddle while John dismounted. John handed the reins to Casey and took Mackenzie from him.

"Make sure to rub Jackson down and call a doctor. Kenzie needs her ankle checked out." Casey nodded and led

Jackson away. "Natalie, I need you to make Kenzie a bowl of soup and some hot chocolate."

"Of course." Natalie held the door open for them and followed behind them to the kitchen. John carried Mackenzie up to their room and placed her on the bed. He started the water in the tub and let it fill up. He went back into the room and helped Mackenzie get undressed. He checked on the water in the tub when someone knocked on the door. He turned off the water and walked to the door.

"Who is it?"

"It's me. Her soup and hot chocolate are ready."

"Thank you, Natalie. Keep them warm until Kenzie is done with her bath." He listened as Natalie walked down the hall. When he heard her go down the stairs, he turned back to Mackenzie, picked her up and placed her in the bathtub, making sure that her hurt ankle wasn't in the water.

He started bathing Mackenzie. He was gentle with her leg, making sure not to bump it.

Mackenzie looked up at John. "John, did you really mean what you said about having kids?" He kissed her on her forehead.

"Of course, I meant it. Kenzie, I love you and would like to give you kids one day. I guess what I am saying is that I want to spend the rest of my life with you. So, Mackenzie Tucker, will you marry me?"

"Oh, John! Yes, I will marry you. I love you, John

Daniels with all my heart!" He picked her up out of the tub, wrapped a towel around her and carried her to the bed. He kissed her as she wrapped her arms around his neck and kissed him back. In that one kiss, she poured out her soul to him, giving him back all that he had given her.